Lynton Viñas: Shadow In the Darkness

(Retelling of a classic tale)

By

J. Wayne Frye

A Novella

This book is written in Canadian English so teachers should apprise students of the difference in spellings. Vocabulary words with definitions are arranged by chapter in the back of the book. It is recommended teachers review the vocabulary words before assigning readings.

Lynton Viñas:
Shadow in the Darkness

TO: The ghost that was always under my bed when I was a child.

And as always, to my muse, Lynton Globa Viñas

Catalogue Number: 2015-2453588

ISBN: 978-1-928183-23-5

Fireside Books – Victoria, British Columbia
Part of the Peninsula Publishing Consortium

J. Wayne Frye

Lynton Viñas: Shadow in the Darkness

TABLE OF CONTENTS

J. Wayne Frye

Lynton Viñas:
Shadow in the Darkness

About the Author

Wayne Frye's *Aaron Adams, Girl* series books and *Lynton* adventures are popular with mystery readers. He provides satirical political commentary to many Canadian newspapers, and his books on politics have created a great deal of controversy. He has written marketing/advertising textbooks, been a highly successful U.S. university hockey coach, professor, university president and served as a marketing consultant to hockey teams and motion picture companies. He has been cited for his work with inner-city gangs in Los Angeles and been active in the anti-globalization movement. He became a Canadian citizen in 2003 and lives in Ladysmith, British Columbia and Laguna, Philippines.

Some Other Books by J. Wayne Frye

Hockey Mania and the Mystery of Nancy Running Elk
Something Evil in the Darkness at Hopkins House
How Hockey Saved a Jew From the Holocaust:
The Rudi Ball Story
The Catastrophic Calamities of a Village Idiot
Fighting for Justice in the Land of Hypocrisy
The Girl Who Stirred up the Whirlwind
The Girl Who Motivated Murder Most Foul
The Girl Who Said Goodbye for the Last Time
Fall From Apocalypse
Armageddon Now
Worth
When Jesus Came to Jersey as the Son of Thunder
When Jesus Came to Canada to Lead an Indigenous Rebellion
Canadian Angels of Mercy – Nurses in Times of Peril
Points of Rebellion: Aboriginals Who Fought for Justice
Lynton Walks on Water
Lynton Curls Her Hair
Lynton and the Vampire at Tagaytay Manor
Lynton Buys a Cell-Phone and Hears the Voice of Doom
Lynton and the Ghosts at the Mansion on Balete Drive
Lynton Viñas and Beowulf Perez: Demon Fighters
Chablis and Lynton in the Room of Doom
Chablis: Avenging Angel for the Forgotten
In the City of Lost Hope
Chablis and the Terrorist
Pursuit
The Disappearance
Lynton's South African Adventure: Demon at the Karoo Escarpment

J. Wayne Frye

Lynton Viñas:
Shadow in the Darkness

PROLOGUE
DARK SHADOW

The darkness is so very, very deep
The curtains flutter with no breeze
Of goblins and ghosts does the dark speak
Fear my young body does seize
Faces with deep, blank eyes stare at me
As they are writhed in the pain of the dead
Oh, I must cover my head not to see
For fear they may feed on me

J. Wayne Frye

Lynton Viñas:
Shadow in the Darkness

As a child, I often had horrible, nightmarish, dark illusions that made me frightened to sleep in the dark. I would leave my light on, lie on my side, pull the covers over my head, just leaving a small opening for my nose so I could breathe more easily, and listen intently to what appeared to be a sawing noise. "Oh my," I would think, there is some demon under my bed trying to saw through my mattress and steal my soul. Night after night, I gasp in fear as I kept hearing that sound, knowing that something evil was after me. I would often cry out, only to be told after my mother looked under the bed, "nothing there. Go to sleep now little scared boy."

I would close my eyes tightly, pull the covers over me for that feeling of safety, and once again hear that horrible, never ending sawing sound. My heart raced and I shivered, knowing that eventually the demon would saw through the mattress and have me.

J. Wayne Frye

Lynton Viñas:
Shadow in the Darkness

As I matured, the covers gradually came off my head. Still, I would hear that eerie sawing sound, but eventually noticed that lying on my back, there would be no noise. I was safe on my back. Gradually, I became adapt at sleeping on my back, which seemed to keep the evil demon at bay night after night. Even into my teenage years, I slept on my back, out of habit, or maybe out of that subconscious fear that the old demon was still under the bed, still waiting to saw through and capture my soul.

One night when I was in my thirteenth year, for some reason I simply could not endure sleeping on my back any longer. I rolled over on my side. My mother came in and looked shocked to see me on my side. She bent over, kissed me goodnight, stopped at the door and looked back. She said, "Are you alright Wayne?"

"Yes," I replied.

Lynton Viñas:
Shadow in the Darkness

She nonchalantly flipped off the light, pulled the door closed and the room was bathed in darkness. I was a teenager now, and I should have had no fear, but I reached down and instinctively pulled the covers up over my head. I peered out into the darkness from the small opening and watched as shadows seemed to dance about the room. Were there more demons coming for me? Had they been waiting all these years just for the right time to pounce on me? Was this the night that their patience would finally get them the soul they sought?

Then it was there. Oh my, I heard it again. Yes, the sawing started. It was back; back to haunt me in the darkness. Steady, methodical, unbroken, the sound penetrating my brain, playing a symphony of horror. It was like symbols clanging, clanging, clanging in my head. I was on the verge of screaming. I was ready to cry out in fear; the terror that had been building all those years was now

J. Wayne Frye

Lynton Viñas:
Shadow in the Darkness

ready to destroy me, ready to consume me and toss me into the dark pit of eternal fire.

I began to shiver. Gradually the shiver became an intense shaking. This was it. This was the night I had dreaded for so long. I could hear it nearing me, nearing the top of the mattress, ready to saw through and devour my soul.

The symphony of evil in my pounding head was reaching a crescendo now - louder, louder and louder. The sawing noise, the infernal sawing noise was becoming faster and more furious. It was as if my head would explode. I wanted to scream but no sound would come out of my throat. I could feel the scream just lying there lodged in fear.

At that moment when I thought all was about to end and that I was finally going to fall prey to that evil demon, I instinctively noticed my eyes

Lynton Viñas:
Shadow in the Darkness

blinking. They were in furious motion, as a result of fear. I began to smile and then laughed. All those years of fear, trepidation and anguish flowed into a river of tranquility. The sawing sound was simply my long eyelashes fluttering against the pillow. That was the sawing sound. That was the demon sawing through my mattress, just my fluttering eyelashes.

I pulled the covers off my head, sighed and drifted off to sleep unafraid. Of course, I did not see the dark shadow at the foot of my bed looking longingly at me.

Lynton Viñas:
Shadow in the Darkness

CHAPTER 1

THE FURY OF THE DEVIL HIMSELF

Go to the gate, sweet Lynton and do not fall
There where the vines cling crimson on the wall,
And in the twilight wait for what will come.
The leaves will whisper there of death, and some,
Like flying words, will strike you as they fall;
But go, and if you listen, evil will call.
Go to the dark gate, sweet Lynton and be brave,
For you have a soul to save.

J. Wayne Frye

Lynton Viñas:
Shadow in the Darkness

No, there is not a dawn in eastern skies
To rift the fiery night that's in lurking eyes;
There, where western glooms are gathering,
The dark will pour upon the dark, if anything:
Good slays itself with every leaf that flies,
And hell is more than half of paradise.
No, there is not a dawn in eastern skies -
In those distant eastern skies.

Out of a grave he comes to tell you this,
Out of a grave he comes to quench the kiss
That flames upon your forehead with a glow,
That blinds you to the way that you must go.
Yes, there is yet one way to where he is,
Bitter, but one that faith may never miss.
Out of a grave he comes to tell you this—
To tell you this.

There is the dark gate, do not fall,
There are the crimson leaves upon the wall,
Go, for the winds are tearing them away,

J. Wayne Frye

Lynton Viñas:
Shadow in the Darkness

Nor think to riddle the dead words they say,

Nor any more to feel them as they fall;

But go, and trust not evil's call.

There by the dark gate, do not fall,

For evil's search will not stall.

There are those who lurk in the shadows and haunt us, usually at night, and primarily when we are children. As we grow up, we tend to put aside the childish fears as we must deal with the fears of reality – the reality that the world is not a very nice place and is filled with those who lurk about, not in the shadows but in the cold light of the day where a world based on greed burdens us with the constant struggle to survive. This world, where the few hold sway over the many, promulgates unfairness and injustice so that the privileged are exalted while the vast majority toil in obscurity. In this world walks a woman of physical and inner beauty who shines the light of hope on all who bask in her presence. This is Lynton Viñas.

Lynton Viñas:
Shadow in the Darkness

As Lynton sat listening to her friend, Charlotte, pour out her fears, she reached over and held her hand, for she knew the meaning of fear. She had faced it often in her demon fighting career, faced the evil head on, never flinching, never wavering in her belief that good trumped evil.

Charlotte had tears in her eyes as she said, "This scares me and I don't know why. I have been seeing them since I was a little girl. Always out of the corner of my eye, a tall black shadow. I always feel like something or someone is by me. Last night it tried to touch me. There it was, standing by my bed when I opened my eyes. I cried, sobbed like a baby I was so frightened. It was so scary. I don't know what it is. I need all the help I can get! That is why I came to you. You are famous as a demon fighter. Can you help me, please?"

"Charlotte, I am not sure I have ever helped anyone. I have been doing this for years and tales

J. Wayne Frye

Lynton Viñas:
Shadow in the Darkness

of walking shadows come from across the world. Some of these shadows wander through the periphery of our lives; others stay for years. People can rarely make out features of these darker-than-night, human shaped entities other than an occasional set of blazing red eyes. Shadow people often appear cloaked, wearing a hat, or bald and sexless. These entities may simply trek through our bedroom at night, never to be seen again, while others may lurk in doorways, just watching, day after day. What are they? Why are they with us? What do they want?"

Charlotte was shaking now. "I thought the end of my childhood was the end of the shadows, but a few days ago, after over 20 years, they came back, haunting me again, making my life a living hell. I thought they were just a childhood phenomena, and they did disappear for so long, but now they are back, and I feel they are coming for me, coming for my soul."

Lynton Viñas:
Shadow in the Darkness

Lynton, though she had seen many things she could not explain, was always a sceptic. She was very measured in her response. "Shadows are thought by many to be demonic entities, ghosts, or other denizens of the dark realm we call the unknown. Regardless of the label, I prefer to think that they are manifestations in our own minds. I do not believe they are real. The mind is a powerful instrument and we often have little control over it. I have studied the paranormal for years, but have arrived at no solid explanations for any of the strange occurrences I have seen or heard about. Whether real or imagined, they are real in our minds, and that is what really counts. I studied the strange occurrences that affected a young boy of 12, who is now 35. Once he was running to the store for his mom. It was overcast but not raining, and in the middle of the afternoon. The day was shadow-less, and decades later he still doesn't know what he saw on his way home from the store, arms laden with food. At first, he thought it

J. Wayne Frye

Lynton Viñas:
Shadow in the Darkness

was a friend. As he approached the corner to turn onto his street, he saw something black sticking out beyond the bushes in the front of his house. He yelled out his friend's name and ran toward the black cloaked figure. He got within a few feet of him and realized it was not his friend. The figure began to grow to an enormous size, turned and ran toward the little boy's house, scampering down the driveway. He frantically ran after it, not fearful, but curious. The black figure did not open the fence gate to the backyard, but just morphed through it and disappeared. To this very time, that experience haunts him, because when he got up to his mother's room, she lay on the bed, dead from suicide, having taken a whole bottle of sleeping pills. He postulated that the black figure was death and had come for his mother. Was it death, or was it just a premonition in the boy's mind that his mother was dead? I cannot answer the question. I can only say that the mind works in ways we simply cannot always understand."

Lynton Viñas:
Shadow in the Darkness

Charlotte leaned forward, put her head in her cupped hands and sobbed. Lynton moved closer and hugged her, held her close to let her know that she cared. "You are not alone in your fears, Charlotte. Others have these experiences, too. "I've been visited by what I presume to be the same shadow three times in my life, and the memories have haunted me on occasion. When I was six, I saw it at my grandfather's house, towering over my bed, almost floating above me. I couldn't move, and I don't remember what happened next. All I remember is trying to scream, but there was this horrible weight on my chest that simply would not let any sound come out. That night my grandfather died in his sleep. Then, I saw the figure again three days before my grandmother died, when I was 12. I walked into the living room late at night and she had fallen asleep watching television. There, standing by the television set was a dark figure, the same floating dark figure. I blinked my eyes and it was gone."

Lynton Viñas:
Shadow in the Darkness

Charlotte said, "And the third time?"

Lynton let a smile creep across her succulent red lips that seemed to be always puckered for a kiss. She licked them. "The third time was at work one day. I was in the back of the salon, putting away some supplies. The light was off and I heard the roar of thunder as a fierce rain storm came up suddenly. As the rain pounded mercilessly on the tin roof I blinked, looked over in a far corner and there it was – that dark figure. What came over me I do not know? I cannot explain it, but I grabbed my umbrella and ran home like the wind. I knew something was wrong. My boyfriend, with whom I was living at the time, was home alone, or so I assumed. Fearful for his life, I bounded into the house, scurrying to the bedroom. I should not have feared. He was in bed with another woman. I grabbed her by the hair and threw her onto front porch, went back in and as he was putting on his clothes, knocked him out with a left hook."

Lynton Viñas:
Shadow in the Darkness

The two women laughed uproariously, as the demure, 5:2, 50 kilos Lynton was certainly not one who would be suspected of fisticuffs. However, underestimating the dynamic dynamo often came at great peril.

It was good to see Charlotte laugh, but it was only a brief respite. Sighing she said, "Surely there must be an explanation for my visions, though?"

"You are not unique, as I have said. Most encounters I have studied are readily explainable. Generally, the persons seeing the dark figures wakes to find a dark, human-like figure standing in the doorway or by the bed, just watching. Tightness grips their chests like the weight of a person is upon them. They can't breathe. Suddenly the choking eases and the shadows are gone. This type of encounter is common, and psychology has a name for it – sleep paralysis."

J. Wayne Frye

Lynton Viñas:
Shadow in the Darkness

"Most psychologists believe these encounters are probably the product of dreams. The fear, the paralysis, and the entities are normal. There are hormones that paralyze the major muscle groups and it's called paradoxical sleep. This is a temporary manifestation, as the people don't stay asleep and the hormones are still in their bodies. It can last for a long time. And, believe it or not, we can be asleep and be walking around, unaware that we are sleeping. When the person becomes fully awake, the shadow encounter is over; all that's left is the fear. Other times these encounters can be attributed to the same trick of light and shadow that allows us to see faces in clouds, trees and buildings. These sightings can also be from electrical stimulation to certain parts of the brain, or drugs. Almost anything can throw off the chemical balance of the brain and cause all sorts of problems. All sensation is in the nervous system and it is all simple chemistry. However, some encounters with shadows occur in full consciousness and full daylight, removing the logical, scientific answers, and leaving something terrible for us to contemplate."

"So," said a pensive Charlotte, sometimes there is no explanation?"

"Of course not, some things defy explanation. My former boyfriend always wanted a light on, because of what happened when he was a child. As a child, he was lying on his bed with the lights on. A shadowy figure emerged from his closet and moved towards his bedside. The shadow reached out a finger and touched his leg. He screamed and the figure vanished, and his folks were there in moments. My boyfriend's father noticed that the closet door was open, and his parents knew he never slept without it closed. They saw a black spot on his leg, a bruise. The shadow being never returned, but he never slept in the dark again, until I knocked him out of course."

Lynton Viñas:
Shadow in the Darkness

They shared another laugh, as Charlotte said, "So, you think these things are a figment of the imagination, but mine seem so real."

"I have made a study of demonology, Charlotte. I am a professed non-believer when it comes to religion, but I do believe in evil. A world where half the people go to bed hungry at night is filled with the evil of greed. A world where religion is used to judge and condemn is an abominable evil. Now, I have a friend who is a Catholic priest. He feels that these shadows must be taken seriously. He believes they are something evil and dangerous. He thinks these things are energy from beyond the grave manifesting physical characteristics they had when living on earth. He believes these entities can move, communicate, and attack, drawing energy from their human victim. I place little credence in his beliefs, but I will share a story with you just as an adjunct to what he believes."

Lynton Viñas:
Shadow in the Darkness

Charlotte was enthralled and listened intently as Lynton continued. "A Wyoming ranch family, all 5 of them, children and adults had been encountering a black, human-shaped figure, featureless except for a wide-brimmed hat, for many years at various places on the ranch – the house, the barn, the cattle pens, the corn field. He first appeared to one of the children when she was 16, terrifying her nightly for almost two years, pacing about her room, as if waiting for something. The entity, with fiery red eyes, never spoke, and never approached her, but she knew why it was there – it hungered, hungered for her. She became convinced it was feeding, absorbing energy from her terror. She was unable to scream, just always transfixed on it as it paced about. The girl went to college far from home and the visits stopped until after she graduated, when she returned home full-time after getting a teaching job in a nearby town. She had to leave for work when it was still dark outside, and one morning as

Lynton Viñas:
Shadow in the Darkness

she was scraping the frost off the car, she glanced at the passenger seat out of the left corner of her eye and there it was – the shadow was sitting in the passenger seat red eyes blazing with fiery evil. It stared at her and she ran into the house, got her mom and dad and when they returned the figure was gone. It was then that her mom told her that she had seen it many times in her own bedroom, usually early in the morning when it was still dark and her husband had left to plough the fields before sun-up. Her two sisters had also had visits in their bedrooms. The mom had also seen it come down the stairs at night, turn into the kitchen and disappear. One night, when her husband was gone, she went to bed with great trepidation, because she had seen the shadow earlier in the day, coming down the stairs. She lay down; trying to drift off to sleep, but she felt an eerie sensation. She looked over in a far corner and there was something - something dark. A strange feeling pulled her upward and she sat up in bed. As she sat in the

Lynton Viñas:
Shadow in the Darkness

dark room, staring at the bedroom wall, she saw it take form. She saw a dark shadow, darker than the night like a void. The figure moved toward the bed and then stopped, standing there motionless. She could only make out the silhouette of his head and shoulders. The rest of him just went straight to the floor. There were no legs or feet, no eyes, no facial features whatsoever. Terrified, she slid low in bed, pulling the covers slowly over her face, watching the black, man-shaped figure standing over her until her blankets hid the horror from view. She shivered in fear until finally drifting off to sleep from exhaustion. The father and mother are long dead now, and the girls sold the ranch. However, the teacher did visit once when the family they sold it to had a daughter who was in her class. As she sat visiting, a sudden scream rang out and they all bounded up the stairs. Her student was at her desk, shaking in horror, crying uncontrollably as she said that a shadow had come out of the closet and beckoned to her. The teacher

Lynton Viñas:
Shadow in the Darkness

left and never returned again, sure that the same shadow was still lurking about."

Charlotte said, "I am so afraid Lynton, so afraid."

"History Charlotte indicates most of these sightings are benign. It is my personal opinion that they are nothing but manifestations conjured up in our minds, caused by events that play upon our psyches."

"Dear Lynton, you are always so calm, so sympathetic in your assessments of situations of stress that plague those of us in despair. I came here for help, and though you have provided no concrete answers, you do give me solace and comfort. Have you never, in all your demon hunting across the globe not come upon that which drove a cold chill throughout your body, made you doubt your own sanity?"

Lynton Viñas:
Shadow in the Darkness

Lynton eased back in her chair, took a deep breath and said, "Oh Charlotte, I am going to share with you that which I have shared with no one else in many years. I have known fear that has coursed through my veins like a Tsunami roaring ashore with the fury of the devil himself."

J. Wayne Frye

CHAPTER 2

THE CHURCH WAS ABOUT MONEY

Writhing with pain

In the darkness

And morphing into screech

At the gnarling shadow show

Grabbed blanket worn with sweat

Warming fear with fears

Piercing screaming swirls

This dark veil disguised

J. Wayne Frye

Lynton Viñas:
Shadow in the Darkness

Shrouding evil entities
In my meandering mind
Will the night never end

Lynton was about to regale Charlotte with a story of shadows, deep, dark shadows of the mind that would dance about in the night like a Mary Shelly nightmare more sinister than her Frankenstein monster. It was a tale she had rarely told to anyone, but, for some reason, she felt compelled to share it on this night.

Lynton had great trepidation, but felt somewhat relieved as she began to share that which had plagued her for so long. The facts which I am about to relate happened to her some ten years ago, at which time she was serving as a trouble shooting manager for a hair salon. She was perpetually on the move and was still young enough to enjoy a life of constant travelling as she had no family ties to speak of.

J. Wayne Frye

Lynton Viñas:
Shadow in the Darkness

There are, indeed, many less agreeable ways in which a person may contrive to scorn delights and live laborious days. You see, Lynton was a person who always enjoyed a challenge, and though she had not, at this time, been given her now famous moniker by Wayne Frye, *the dynamic dynamo*, she was certainly that even before he made her famous in his books. In remote places, where strangers are scarce, her annual visit to the salon in Nangalisan, which is near the urban area of Baguio in northern Luzon in the Philippines, was not cause of concern for those who worked there, as they always appreciated her kind way of showing them how to improve on their performances. The tiny town was a delight for her, since it was a centre for Buddhist culture, which befitted her more laissez-faire attitude in regards to religion. She jokingly said, "I have no time for religion. I prefer to be nonjudgmental, and for me, religion too often had rather condemn and ridicule rather than lift people up from despair."

Lynton Viñas:
Shadow in the Darkness

She had a long walk from the bus terminal on the outskirts of Baguio, but being the coolest place in the Philippines because of the altitude, she was enjoying her walk in the cool evening breeze. She loved the little village where the salon was, because she always enjoyed the light conversation and banter with the townspeople, especially at the country inn. She was a most agreeable person, and had formed many friendships there over the years.

The village was a rambling, thinly populated area and breathtakingly beautiful. No doubt, nature serves as the biggest source of inspiration to people. And mountains, in particular, are one of the most beautiful forms that nature can ever take. But this little town lying at the foot of a mountain was a perfect combination of nature and civilization that go hand in hand together with so much beauty and simplicity that it always took her breath away. It was intersected at right angles by two ranges of barren hills and cut off to a large

J. Wayne Frye

Lynton Viñas:
Shadow in the Darkness

extent from the main lines of transportation. The noisy smoke belching Jeepneys that are so common in the Philippines were banned, along with motorized tricycles and all cars had to be parked at municipal lots outside the main village. This was indeed a haven for peacefulness and serenity in a land where traffic jams, deplorable pollution and grinding poverty were so prevalent. There was poverty there, but by virtue of the village's smallness and commitment to lifting up all who resided within, it was more tolerable and less of an eye sore, as residents seemed to all take pride in the place they called home.

There were several villages in the valley and they lay wide apart, often separated by long tracts of rice paddies; and as Lynton was walking between villages, she looked up at the towering mountain, which was an extinct volcano and saw a dark cloud above the summit. It seemed not to move, just hang there in the darkening day.

Lynton Viñas:
Shadow in the Darkness

Winter, which was the wet month, was near at hand, as she made her way to the village proper. A few tricycles passed her on the way, and recognizing her, many of the passengers in the side cars waved a cheerful hello. She had just seen the sign for Pittsfield, a place she had often passed but never ventured into the village proper. It was a hilly cross-roads between her and the journey's end. She had often made enquiries about the place, but all in the town of Nangalisan seemed reluctant to talk of the neighbouring village. In fact, they seemed to always change the subject when questions about Pittsfield came up.

For some reason, curiosity this day got the better of her, and rather than stay at her normal bed and breakfast, she decided to venture into Pittsfield. She turned to her right and started walking toward the village. Her walk soon ended at a place called Balette Road, whence a rickety old Jeepney picked her up and conveyed her, along with four other

J. Wayne Frye

Lynton Viñas:
Shadow in the Darkness

drab looking passengers toward the village. The bouncy ride was most disconcerting, as the Jeepney driver possessed that rather common propensity among such untrained drivers for racing the engine constantly which caused a jerking motion. She was considering shouting "intigil" so he would stop and let her out, as surely, she surmised, walking would be better than enduring the insanity of this driver who obviously was prepping for next Memorial Day's Indianapolis 500. Still, the now arrived night was very dark with only two or three stars twinkling above and she was unfamiliar with the road into town, so she decided to endure the miseries she had endured so many years riding in Jeepneys. This was simply part of her culture that she did not particularly embrace, but in a nation that refused to tax the rich and corporations, there simply were few municipalities that offered any decent public transportation. This was the price of unfettered capitalism with no constraints.

Lynton Viñas:
Shadow in the Darkness

She surmised that she had miscalculated the distance to town as the way lay over a succession of long hills, rising to a barren, high-level plateau. She turned to a fellow passenger and asked, "How much further to town?" The passenger just stared at her, not answering. It was then that Lynton noticed the other passengers, like the one to whom she addressed the question, seemed totally mute, almost as if none had the ability to speak. They all had deep, dark-set eyes and they seemed to be staring into the darkness with a deep longing. They did not seem to be breathing as their chests were not rising or falling. She decided to address the question to the Jeepney driver, and when she did she got the fright of her life as an almost skeleton like face, with a hood over its head, peered back at her with eyes that were as fiery red as one might expect the smouldering embers of hell to be, and he said, as slamming on his brakes, screeching to a halt and pointing to his right, "There it is, you can walk the rest of the way."

Lynton Viñas:
Shadow in the Darkness

Only too happy to be free of the Jeepney and its eerie inhabitants, Lynton was delighted to walk the rest of the way; and, she set off at a good pace, leaving the driver and rickety pile of junk Jeepney behind. She turned to look back, and the Jeepney was gone, as if it had disappeared into thin air. "Well," she thought, "the way he was driving it is no surprise he scurried down the road quickly." Yet, she did not hear the engine race, and she saw no lights from the rear of the Jeepney as one would expect.

Again, she looked up at the mountain summit, and the cloud still hung there, seemingly not having moved at all. She saw some faint lights in the near distance and found a footpath that led across a barren slope divided by stone fences, with here and there a group of old stone sheds, a tall chimney that was, no doubt, at one time a potter's kiln, and a blackened mound, marking the dumping ground of the cinders from the fires. A

Lynton Viñas:
Shadow in the Darkness

light fog, meanwhile, was creeping up behind, and the few stars that had once lit her way were now covered by clouds. Thus, she became concerned with losing her way in the almost total darkness that was engulfing her.

Now, to lose one's way in such a place and at such an hour would be disagreeable enough, and the footpath, which was a trodden track already half obliterated, would be indistinguishable in the course of another few minutes as the fog was now rolling in from all sides. Looking anxiously ahead; therefore, in the hope of seeing some sign of habitation, she hastened on quickly at a feverous pace. The lights ahead were beginning to fade in the thickening fog and behind her; she sensed something moving in her direction. The cold was now beginning to settle in, and she reached down in her huge bag she was carrying, instinctively looking for her jacket, but alas, she realized she had forgotten to pack it. Presently, she came to a

J. Wayne Frye

point where the path divided; where she was confused about which one to take, but since they both seem to head toward the distant lights; she elected to go right, assuming it didn't really matter.

Our lives are filled with paths. The history of humanity has, to a large extent, been one of groping blindly in the dark, looking for the right path while fearing for the future and yet resisting the fear that we are on the wrong road. Unfortunately, far too often, the wrong path is selected. That night, Lynton was beginning to wonder if she had made the wrong choice, as the fog engulfed her now, surrounding her in pitch blackness as she again heard that faint noise behind her. This was not a woman who was prone to hysterics or any fear whatsoever, but this night she felt a chill run up and down her spine. What was behind her? It did not sound like footsteps; rather it was just a feeling something was there.

Lynton Viñas:
Shadow in the Darkness

Where was she headed? Why had she chosen to do this? What had motivated her to go to this village, rather than stay at her usual place? Was there some unseen force compelling her to be in this place at this time? Had she taken the wrong path?

The feeling something was behind her was overwhelming now. Still, she trod forward with determination. There was no time to be lost in hesitation; so she moved briskly now, still sensing there was something behind her. She looked to her left, and there beside her was a man moving quickly past her. Up to this moment she had not met a living soul of whom to ask her way; it was, therefore, with no little sense of relief that she saw the man emerging from the fog behind her and coming along the path. As he neared her side, advancing rapidly; she slowly observed that he was dragging his left foot, limping as he walked. It was, however, so dark and so misty, that not until

J. Wayne Frye

he was close enough to touch her could she see that he wore a dark cloak, and had a hood over his head to where she could not make out his facial features.

She turned toward him as they both continued walking and said, "Am I on the right path to the Pittsfield?"

He never slowed, never hesitated at all, as looking straight before him; he took no notice of the question; apparently not hearing it. So, she said, this time raising her voice, "I beg your pardon sir, but will this path take me to the village?"

He continued straight ahead, without pausing, not once even looking her way. His stride quickened and the dragging foot was now being pulled along furiously as Lynton stepped up her pace, but could not keep up.

Lynton Viñas:
Shadow in the Darkness

Finally, as he faded into the thickening fog, she stopped, stood still bewildered for a few seconds contemplating the strangeness of it all. She decided to follow him, but he was completely gone into the fog now. He had totally disappeared. Then, there coming toward her out of the thick fog was a shadowy figure with a slender pole in his hand. He was a tall lad who was half-walking, half-running. She recognized the slender pole as a fishing rod that was resting partly on his shoulder. He was completely quiet, and seemed to make no noise whatsoever as he walked briskly toward her. And surely he had run into the man in the cloak as they were on the same path. She stopped, stood dumbfounded and as the figure approached, she said, "Hello there my boy. I am lost."

He said not a word. He did not even acknowledge her presence. Like the man, he appeared to not hear her as he moved right past her and continued into the fog.

Lynton Viñas:
Shadow in the Darkness

As he moved into the darkness she shouted. "Hello there, hello!" He did not tarry, only continued onward until he, like the other, disappeared into the fog.

Her stupefaction was such that she stood quite still, looking into the darkness. Was she dreaming? Shaking her head in disbelief, she realized it mattered not whether she was dreaming or not, she had to press on. She hurried forward, plunging deeper into the fog at every step. She was; however, close upon the journey's end. The path ended at a wide opening onto an old cobblestone road that led down a steep lane; and at the bottom of the lane, down which she nearly stumbled among stones and ruts, she came in sight of the welcome glare of a lights in what appeared to be an inn of some type. Here then, was the village at last. She pressed forward and there before her stood a tall man in the doorway of the inn actually beckoning her toward him.

Lynton Viñas:
Shadow in the Darkness

"Not a fit night for a young lady to be out, ma'am. Come on in for a drink to warm you and maybe a room if you need one."

The Grey Goose was a modest hotel where she shared a little parlour with a couple of sales representatives and a young man who informed her that she was an unusually beautiful woman. Feeling relieved, she dined, pulled out her cellphone and was able to use the Wi-Fi, chatted awhile with the inn's owner, and picked up such scraps of local news in regards to a recent apparent disappearance, which many surmised had actually occurred along the very path which Lynton had taken. A young woman had ventured out to visit relatives in Nangalisan and simply disappeared two weeks ago and had not been seen since. It was assumed that she had simply strayed from the path and perhaps lost her way, succumbing to some wild predators in the dense jungle nearby. It had happened to others before.

J. Wayne Frye

Lynton Viñas:
Shadow in the Darkness

Also present was the town priest who was enthusiastically working on his weekly church sermon. The priest was cordial enough, but was a bit too direct when he asked Lynton if she was a regular churchgoer. When she replied, "no," he sat up straighter in his chair, stiffing his back and gave her a look of indignation. She, never one to cower before the church hierarchy, which she looked upon as nothing more than executives in just another corporation, said, "I gave up on the church since it continues to ignore the abject poverty of the country and the growing gap between the haves and have-nots. It seems to me it needs a bit of social conscience."

The priest got up, looked down at her with disdain and walked over to the bar, ordering a glass of wine. Lynton smiled, as she enjoyed letting the clergy know that she saw them as servants to the privileged class. She was not one to every bow in supplication before authority.

Lynton Viñas:
Shadow in the Darkness

Looking at a picture on the wall, Lynton recognized the man in the photos as an old friend from high school days. She asked the innkeeper if he knew the person in the photo. He replied, "Of course, he owns this building. He is a very successful young man. He lives here only part time, as he is a world traveller. He is home right now, lives at the far end of the village in the three story mansion overlooking the entire village. I think he is due to leave us next week, going to Japan on business I think."

"So, Mr. Robert Chavez lives here, very interesting."

"You know him?"

"I do. We were classmates at Cambridge School of Law - a very nice person."

"Indeed. He is a fine gentleman."

Lynton Viñas:
Shadow in the Darkness

Lynton, curious, asked, "How long has he lived here?"

"Oh, for maybe close to 10 years at least, though he is gone most of the time. He spends much of his time in a place called Overton, which is near Baguio, just north of it. He has another home there, and I am told it is a grand place, like a palace."

"Overton," Lynton thought. The name was not new to her; she had heard it before, but could not remember where. The innkeeper, who finally introduced himself as Richard Sanchez, heaped a great deal of praise on Robert Chavez as a true gentleman and grand landlord, whom, he thought was alone way too much.

Lynton reflected on her time at the Cambridge School of Law, where she remembered Robert and his friend Blackman Perez were always asking her

Lynton Viñas:
Shadow in the Darkness

for a date. They were both very cute, but she had no romantic interest in either and always said, "No."

She remembered Robert Chavez so well. He had a handsome face, was always fastidiously dressed, had a boyish prodigality that often bordered on utter indolence, and he had a cadre of blind faith worshippers, who believed that he was a prince among men. He was arrogant but still charming, and he left college with the reputation of having narrowly escaped expulsion for some of his shenanigans. How vividly it all came back to Lynton, who was not surprised at how he had apparently finessed his way about Pittsfield and mesmerized all there with his charm. It had been but eleven years since Lynton had seen him; yet it seemed like half a century. And now, after those eleven years, she took a different path on her way to Nangalisan, and here she was staring up at his picture in an building that he owned.

Lynton Viñas:
Shadow in the Darkness

She wondered if he was much changed, and whether, if changed, if it were for the better or the worse. Had his frivolous, flighty ways developed into sterling virtues, or had his follies hardened into vices? Should she let him know she was in town and so judge for herself if he wanted to meet? Nothing would be easier than to pencil a line upon a card in the morning, and send it up to the big house. Yet, merely to satisfy a purposeless curiosity, was it worthwhile to reopen the acquaintanceship? Thus musing, she sat late in the lounge area, and by the time she went to bed, she had well forgotten the strange occurrence on the path with the man who vanished so mysteriously and the boy who seemed to come from nowhere.

Next morning, finding she had abundant time at her disposal since it was Sunday, she did pencil that line upon her business card, reminding him of whom she was, as if anyone could forget Lynton. And then, having dispatched it by one of the

Lynton Viñas:
Shadow in the Darkness

workers at the inn, she decided to walk over to Nangalisan to say hello to the workers at the salon and warn them she would be there on Monday.

The day was brilliantly fine. The wind was blowing steadily in her face as she made her way over the path. The sun shone clear but the altitude in the area made it cold for the Philippines, and the village began to disappear behind her as she moved steadily along. The whole area skirted a long hill-side, with the church and school being at the top of a small mesa. Looking vainly for the lane by which she had come the night before, she climbed the one rambling street, followed a path that skirted the churchyard, and found herself at the local graveyard with old tombstones worn and broken all about. There were several hovels that passed as homes all along the periphery of the graveyard, and there was an iron railing and a gate separating the homes from the graves. How convenient thought Lynton, the poor live in

J. Wayne Frye

Lynton Viñas:
Shadow in the Darkness

desperation and they are kept near that which offers them a respite from poverty – death.

She heard a soft voice behind her say, "Appalling that people must live this way, but that is the way of the world. Were there no poor people to exploit there would be no rich, for the rich get that way on the backs of the poor."

She turned, and found the speaker at her elbow, a square-built, tall man, all in black, with a bundle of books under his arm. "I am Mr. Benez, teacher here."

Lynton, always quick with a quip, said, "Ah, the imparter of knowledge to the young furtive minds that must be planted with the seeds of learning that bear the noblest fruit."

Smiling he replied, "Yes, but I think that may be a bit of an embellishment."

Lynton Viñas:
Shadow in the Darkness

"Well, I like to give credit to those who impart wisdom to young minds, because it is the young mind that may change the world from a place where greed is aggrandized as an enviable trait to one where the bounty is shared equally."

"Ah, I know you. You are Lynton Viñas, known to rattle a few cages where the privileged class wall themselves off from the peasants. It is an honour to meet one so young who is dedicated to the betterment of humanity, particularly the poor."

Lynton was thinking to herself that she had seen this man somewhere before, but she could not recall where. "Have I not seen you before?" asked Lynton.

The words were commonplace enough, but the man's manner was studiously, disagreeably deferential, almost as if he resented the question. Then, it became crystal clear where she had seen

J. Wayne Frye

him. His outline, his posture, his very demeanour, the deep, dark-set eyes, the hooded cloak he had on made it obvious. He was the man in the fog.

He stared at her and said, "What is it?"

"I saw you last night in the fog, spoke to you, but you ignored me as if I was not there."

"Last night?"

"You did not seem to observe me, I spoke to you, in fact; but you did not reply to me. You ignored me completely I tell you."

"I beg your pardon. You are mistaken. I was not out at all last night."

How could this be anything but a falsehood, thought Lynton? She might have been mistaken as to the man's face, as it was beneath a hood. Then, she looked down at his feet, moved away from him and said, "Walk to me."

Confused, he shuffled forward, dragging his right foot, as he said, "Why, why do you want me to do this?"

She was now more convinced than ever that it was he whom she had seen in the fog since he was dragging his foot behind him just as the man did. As he stopped right in front of her, he said, "Too damp and too foggy. I did not go out at all last night I tell you."

Lynton took an immediate disliking to the man. There was something sinister going on she thought as the man was heaping lie upon lie but to serve what ends? Why lie about it? Why not just say he was preoccupied and had no time to stop? The matter was extremely perplexing, but she elected to simply let it pass.

Lynton Viñas:
Shadow in the Darkness

Just at that time, a group of kids came running out of church. They ran up to Mr. Benez, and seemed to be highly respectful of him. Whatever his shortcomings as a man of honesty, he certainly did not seem to lack the respect of his students.

The priest to whom Lynton had spoken the previous night was standing in the church doorway and looking toward her. He motioned for her to come to him. A bit rude she thought as he could just as easily come to her, but there was a certain arrogance about those with authority, seeming to think others were supposed to be deferential toward them. She shrugged her shoulders, excused herself from Mr. Benez and walked toward the church.

The priest was actually cordial, saying, "How good to see you. Remember me, Father Mendez. I am afraid I might have come off as rude last night. Please accept my apology."

Lynton Viñas:
Shadow in the Darkness

Lynton replied, "No problem, I can be a bit abrasive myself when it comes to religion Father. I am afraid I am very opinionated when it comes to my feelings about religion."

"No problem. We are all entitled to our opinions, but I would like to ask a favour of you, not for the church, but for the children who play here," and then he pointed toward a dilapidated playground between the church and the school as he continued, "your help with what is a deteriorating playground between the church and the school would be appreciated. You see, we have asked Mr. Chavez for help, but he has ignored our pleas. I hear you are an old classmate of his. I was wondering if you might speak to him about it, perhaps you would have some sway."

Wanting something thought Lynton. What's new in the world of religion? Like everything else in a capitalist society, the church was about money.

CHAPTER 3

I SAW NO ONE

He leaves not a trace, only a shadow you see,
But when he comes by he stares always at me.
His dark eyes; like flowers with frostbite they be
So haunted, not sparkling, no trace left of glee.

Scary in black, won't you tell me your name,
Or tell me at least if you are playing a game.
Did fate break your heart or did you find a dame?

J. Wayne Frye   57

Lynton Viñas:
Shadow in the Darkness

Who suited you more, tell me, who is to blame?

The blackness of him; it is worthy of song,
But chilly! You shiver when he comes along,
And like all his kind - it's not here they belong.
He saves speech and keeps guard on the tongue.

I once met a shadow on the coast,
And of this shadow I now boast.
But was it his soul he had lost?
His heart was covered with frost.

A shadow in black without a name,
An icy-cold heart he had, who to blame?
Are you dead and for me want the same?
Oh, the black shadow for me came.

Profusely apologizing, Father Mendez begged Lynton to use whatever influence she had as the children needed a nice place to play. The children, he said, were allowed to play in the quadrangle, which was too small, and in various ways inconvenient; but round at the back there was a piece of waste land, half an acre of which, if enclosed, would admirably answer the purpose. So saying, he led the way to the back of the building, and Lynton followed him.

Thinking that this was indeed a noble cause, one which the church should do more of rather than concerning itself with the mundane, Lynton was actually interested in helping if she could as she said, "And this ground belongs to Mr. Chavez."

"Yes."

"I have not seen him in years."

"Yes," replied the priest, now seeming less arrogant. "Yet, you are a well-known and respected person. Many have heard of your commitment to social justice. I am sure you want

Lynton Viñas:
Shadow in the Darkness

to help if you can, and obviously this land is of no real value to Mr. Chavez, who has more than any one man needs."

"What reason does he give for not donating the land?"

"None," he replied with a deceptive look.

Lynton looked to her right, and there at the far corner of the church, in the distance, a thin, sinister looking dark shadow appeared to be peering around the corner of the church through the morning mist. It was apparently a person in a long black cloak that covered the head. She could not tell whether it was a man or woman. She turned to the priest and said, "Who is that staring at us over there?"

As Father Mendez turned to look with her, he said, "what person?"

J. Wayne Frye

Lynton Viñas:
Shadow in the Darkness

There was no one there. In the blink of an eye, the shadow had disappeared. Lynton, not wanting to belabour the issue, simply said, "It seemed to me there was someone there. It was more of a shadow than a person. I just wonder why he or she was so obviously staring with interest at the two of us."

"Someone staring," he replied. "I see no one. Why would someone stare at us? Perhaps it was the sun and a cloud above causing an illusion."

The school faced due north, and they were standing immediately behind the buildings, with backs to the sun. The place was bare, and open, and high; and their shadows, sharply defined, lay stretched before their feet.

"Shadow? Perhaps you are the victim of what so many here see from time to time. You are not the first one to see cloaked figures. Many have seen

Lynton Viñas:
Shadow in the Darkness

them. It is a phenomena that is reported by reliable sources from time-to-time. I have never seen anything myself, but others have."

"It isn't important Father Mendez," offered Lynton. She continued. "Do you know Mr. Benez well?"

"I do. He is a kindly teacher, very dedicated to the children."

"Good to hear," replied Lynton as she looked again in the direction where she had seen the dark shadow. There was not a bush or a tree within 100 metres of the spot. There was not a cloud in the sky, despite what Father Mendez had intonated. There was nothing, absolutely nothing that could have cast a shadow. She admitted to herself that it was impossible and that she must have seen an illusion; and so went back to the matter of the playground and promised that if she saw Robert

Lynton Viñas:
Shadow in the Darkness

Chavez, she would mention the playground to him, but that she could promise very little.

"I am much obliged to you," he said but did not sound sincere. Was he somehow toying with her?

Then, Lynton saw it again – the shadow. "Look there!" she interrupted. "It is that shadow."

By the same wall, lying in the full sunlight, their two shadows could be seen against the far wall and there, too, longer and more sinister looking between their shadows, but a little way apart, as if the intruder were standing slightly behind the corner of the building, as sharply defined as a shadow could be, Lynton distinctly saw the menacing looking shadow, though only for a split moment. As she was about to point it out to the father, it was gone again.

"Did you not see it?" she asked.

Lynton Viñas:
Shadow in the Darkness

He shook his head emphatically, as he said with what seemed unsure conviction, "No, I saw nothing. What was it?" Yet, his pallor turned pale. He was even slightly shaking.

"But you must have seen it!" Lynton exclaimed. "It fell just there by the corner of the building - where that bit of ivy grows. There must be someone hiding from out view, staring at us. I am sure of it. Perhaps it is one of the youths from the church, lingering about after dismissal."

"A shadow, there would be no reason for anyone to spy upon us."

Mr. Benez suddenly appeared, seemingly from out of nowhere. "Ah, Father Mendez, I assume you are requesting our friend here to intercede with Mr. Chavez and see if we might procure the property for an extension of the playground." Looking at Lynton he continued, "A noble cause."

Lynton Viñas:
Shadow in the Darkness

She was now bewildered by the appearance and reappearance of the shadow. Looking directly now at Mr. Benez, she said, "Have you seen anything strange over there by the far corner of the church wall?"

Father Mendez offered Mr. Benez an explanation. "She keeps seeing a sinister shadow appear and reappear."

"Ah," offered Benez, "that seems a constant around here. Shadows in the darkness usually though, not the daylight."

Without hesitation, Lynton moved toward the far wall as the two men instinctively followed her. She searched backwards and forwards in every direction. Mr. Benez, with his scared face, was limping at her heels, as Father Mendez, a look of consternation on his face, was scampering about too, but there was no one there by the corner.

Lynton Viñas:
Shadow in the Darkness

Both men looked a bit discombobulated, as Lynton said, "I saw something here I tell you. There was a dark shadow. Someone was behind this corner."

Benez said, "And you saw me last night? I am afraid you must be overwrought about something in your life, maybe making your mind play tricks on you."

She realized she was getting nowhere, because their looks belied their words. She felt positive that they had not only seen the shadow, but that they knew more about it than they chose to tell. She was growing frustrated, wondering if she was being made the object of a prank, and being hoodwinked by the connivance of the two. It was an insult to her intelligence. She said nothing more, just shrugged her shoulders, turned and walked back toward the inn. She was not going to Nangalisan, not yet.

Lynton Viñas:
Shadow in the Darkness

As she neared the bottom of the hill and headed toward the inn, a handsome man with regal bearing was walking briskly toward her. Robert Chavez was impeccably dressed and displayed a flair of cosmopolitan charm, though they were in the back-country. Looking not a day older than when she last saw him at Cambridge, he gripped her by both hands, and insisted she check out of the inn and stay at his place.

In vain she said that she needed to be in Nangalisan on business, but he would hear none of it. He laughed dismissively and irreverently, took her into the establishment, and told her to text the salon and simply say she had other affairs that needed attending to in Pittsfield. How thought Lynton can one possibly argue with such a forceful man? And with this, in his masterful way, he shouted to the landlord to have all her bags sent up to the estate, but she was forceful too and said to leave them right where they were. However,

Lynton Viñas:
Shadow in the Darkness

they did rattle off briskly toward his estate. The magnificent house glistening in the afternoon sun, seemed to dominate the landscape. Still it stood high in the midst of a sombre looking forested area. An avenue of palm trees led up to the house; and a mournful melancholia seemed to permeate all about as the squeaky gate was slowly opened by Robert. Lynton looked at the name on the gate and felt a cold chill run up and down her spine – *Black Raven Manor*.

The place, in fact, was a palatial mansion, but there was a dark sombreness to it. Lynton was taken through the picture gallery and reception rooms after lunch, and then for a walk around the grounds; and in the evening they dined at the upper end of a great bamboo hall where hung the heads of animals he had shot on his many safaris, and there was old armour, and antiquated weapons of warfare and sport. It represented ostentatious disregard for humanity in Lynton's mind.

J. Wayne Frye

Lynton Viñas:
Shadow in the Darkness

"Now, tomorrow," said her host, as they sat on the back balcony over looking the grounds, "if we have decent weather, you shall have a day hiking up the mountain, and on Tuesday, if you will but be persuaded to stay a day longer, I will drive you over to Baguio and give you a tour of my winery there. Then, we'll go into the mines where stalactites and stalagmites dance in a golden display that will dazzle you."

"You own mines, too?"

"I do, several copper mines hereabouts. I guess you could say I am a ruler of the underworld. Outside Baguio the whole area is honeycombed with shafts. One of the richest seams runs under this house, and there are upwards of forty men at work in it one-half kilometre below our feet here every day. Sometimes you can hear a slight vibration when they are blasting. Another seam leads right under the church and school."

Lynton Viñas:
Shadow in the Darkness

"I had no idea in school that you were so rich."

He shrugged his shoulders as he said, "Rich I suppose, but it is always a matter of degrees. I am rich enough to commit what follies I please; and that is saying a good deal. But then, to be always squandering money-always rambling about the world, always gratifying the impulse of the moment, is that happiness? I have been trying the experiment since leaving school; and with what result? Would you like to see?"

He hopped up and led the way through a long suite of unfurnished rooms, the floors of which were piled high with packing cases of all sizes and shapes, labelled with the names of various foreign ports and the addresses of foreign agents innumerable. What did they contain? Precious marbles from Italy and Greece and Asia Minor; priceless paintings by old and modern masters; antiquities from the Nile, the Tigris, and the

J. Wayne Frye

Lynton Viñas:
Shadow in the Darkness

Euphrates; rugs from Persia, porcelain from China, bronzes from Japan, strange sculptures from Peru; armaments, mosaics, wood-carvings, skins, tapestries, old Italian cabinets, terracottas; treasures of all countries, of all ages, never even unpacked as they were of little significance to someone who had so much. He turned to her and said, "There is no pleasure in this. It is treasure but to me worthless."

They sat up late that first night, as Lynton did most of the listening for Chavez did most of the talking, while Lynton, willing to be amused, led him on to tell her something of his wanderings throughout the world. Though it might have appeared exciting to many, she could not help but decipher that he was principally bored with it all, and that there was something he was hiding.

So the time passed in stories of adventure, of perilous peaks ascended, of deserts traversed, of

Lynton Viñas:
Shadow in the Darkness

unknown ruins explored, of hair-raising escapes from catastrophe, earthquakes, storms; and when at last he deeply sighed as if he was bored with the whole conversation and suggested they be off to bed, as he had actually had her bags delivered from the inn. She decided to stay.

Next day, according to the programme, they did all the things he had suggested and finally decided to explore an old Spanish fort. The day tired her out and she slept late the next morning when one of the maids came in to awaken her. She offered her clothes for descending into the mines, and she dressed hurriedly.

The maid was precise and laid out the garments in an orderly fashion as if she were laying out grand ball gowns for a formal evening. She mentioned that other garments might be worn under the clothes she laid out as it was very cold in the mines.

J. Wayne Frye

Lynton Viñas:
Shadow in the Darkness

The morning was overcast, and the prospect of being lowered into the bowels of the earth was anything but attractive. Yet, she felt overwhelmingly compelled to go along with him as he appeared so excited to be sharing the adventures with her. She had not the heart to tell him she was bored to tears.

Hesitatingly, she got up, donned the clothes and went downstairs. A murmur of voices met her ear as she drew near the breakfast-room. Going in, she found some men, obviously mining engineers grouped around the table where Chavez, looking somewhat serious, appeared to be contemplating something as he snapped out of his thought process to introduce Lynton. He did not bother to introduce the men by name just said, "These are some of my engineers."

"Look here, Fernandez," he said, with a short laugh, "a fissure is dangerous, but we cannot halt production. My investors are depending on deliveries."

A bulky man at the end of the table sighed and replied, "It is too dangerous I tell you, way too dangerous. There is almost seven feet of water in the shaft. It will take days to drain it."

Seeming dismayed, but resigned to doing as they suggested, Chavez said, "Do as you will then, but do it fast and efficiently with minimal cost. We cannot delay for long."

So saying, he dismissed the men with a good-humoured nod. Lynton was assured by him that there should be no cause for alarm. Yes, sometimes, instead of merely cracking, the ground would cave in, burying not merely houses, but whole hamlets in one common ruin. The foundations of such houses were, however, generally known to be insecure long enough

Lynton Viñas:
Shadow in the Darkness

before the crash came; and these accidents were not therefore often followed by loss of life.

He told her that he must oversee the operation, but that he would love her to come with him. She did. An entire lake above ground had seemingly collapsed into the mine, so he took Lynton to view the scene of the catastrophe. The way lay far from the house across a wooded upland, beyond which they followed a broad plain. Just as they entered the lake area with Chavez rattling on, a tall, slender boy-like shadow, with something across his shoulder, came out from one of the side paths to the right, crossed at an angle, and disappeared among the trees on the opposite side. Lynton recognized the form instantly. It was the boy whom she saw the other day, just after meeting the cloaked schoolteacher on her way to the village.

"That shadowy figure seems intent on going to the lake despite its precipitous drainage," said

Lynton Viñas:
Shadow in the Darkness

Lynton, happy that now someone else could definitely, without question, see the shadow she had encountered earlier. She continued, "He had some type pole slung over his left shoulder."

"What figure?" asked Chavez, looking in the same direction as Lynton.

"The shadowy figure of what was obviously a boy who just crossed to the right of us, over there," she said as she pointed in the direction where she had seen him before he disappeared into the clump of trees.

Seemingly bewildered, Chavez said, "A boy crossed over there, near those trees, carrying some type pole?"

"Surely you saw him?" pleaded Lynton.

"No, I saw no one."

J. Wayne Frye

CHAPTER 4

WAS IT AN ILLUSION

Footsteps echo in the dark
Howling dogs sinisterly bark
Whispering winds seem to chatter
Ah, there is the shadow of matter

The shadow is there in the dark
On my soul it leaves its mark
The shadow casts strange doubt

J. Wayne Frye 77

Lynton Viñas:
Shadow in the Darkness

What can this evil be about

There is no earthly sound
Can no sanity be found
The shadow is menacing there
Will it pull me into its lair

Lynton was obviously perturbed that now three people had denied seeing shadows that she had seen. She exclaimed, "You did not see the young boy over by the trees? You could not miss him. I mean I saw the shadow of him cast upon the ground as he walked slightly stooped over carrying something on his shoulder. The darkness by the trees shielded his figure, but...."

Chavez interrupted before she could finish. He shook his head as he looked in the direction where Lynton saw the young boy's shadow and said, "Again, I saw nothing. I am sorry but I simply did not see a thing over there."

J. Wayne Frye

Lynton Viñas:
Shadow in the Darkness

Lynton had now encountered the shadowy figure twice, and the second time others should have seen them but did not. What was going on?

"You are dreaming!" Chavez said. "No living thing, not even an animal, has crossed our path since we left the house."

Now even more flustered, Lynton exclaimed, "I am not in the habit of dreaming with my eyes open."

He laughed, and put his arm on her shoulder. "I do not doubt you my dear. It is just that I saw nothing at all."

"There is something strange going on."

"And something beautiful," interjected Chavez as he pulled her closer to him, but Lynton was concentrating on the now apparent illusions that

Lynton Viñas:
Shadow in the Darkness

seemed to be becoming regular occurrences. What did they mean? Could she, in truth, be having hallucinations? She became perplexed, and looking up at Chavez, said, "I am not prone to hysterics, but I have seen things apparently not there twice now."

Chavez took her by the arm and pulled her along. "Don't worry about illusions, look over there," he said as he pointed toward a very unusual looking small lake to their left. They walked about thirty minutes toward the lake. As they arrived, they noticed it was filled with black slime. There was a crowd of people gathered around its periphery.

As Chavez approached, a hush fell over the crowd. They stared intently at him as he nodded greetings to individuals while passing them, as he and the troubled Lynton moved toward a group of his workers.

Lynton Viñas:
Shadow in the Darkness

He had pleasant words for everyone he passed, sharing a nice smile. He stopped at the small lake's edge and said, "Oh my, what a deplorable sight."

An older man, standing nearby, offered a cogent observation. "A damn sorry sight indeed, sir. But there is something uglier than this slime," he said as he pointed to what appeared to be a fishing pole standing straight up in the slime near the shore, and reaching out from the dark slime were two hands gripping the pole.

Lynton gasped for breath, because she had seen the figure carrying something over its shoulder. Could it have been a fishing pole? It had only been a few minutes. Had he walked into the slime and drowned?

Chavez motioned for his workers to retrieve the body from the slime. Two men waded in and they reached deep into the slime, slowly moving toward the pole and the two hands grasping it. They moved steadily forward with muscular efforts by which each step was gained. They were yet full ten metres from the goal when the mud mounted to their armpits, a few feet more, and only their heads would remain above the surface!

Uneasiness ran through the crowd and a lady shouted, "Call them back before they are lost in the muck."

But at the moment of her plea, having reached a point where the ground gradually sloped upwards-they began to rise above the mud as rapidly as they had sunk into it. And then, black with clotted slime, they emerged waist-high within reach of the pole. They grabbed under the slime and slowly pulled, but the body would not budge. It was too heavy for them, so a third party jumped in and made his way to them to assist.

Lynton Viñas:
Shadow in the Darkness

Try as hard as the three could, the corpse would not budge. One of them grabbed the pole as if it was somehow important, and the three edged their way back to shore.

They had not much to tell standing, all mud from head to heel, on dry land again, but one thing was conclusive. It was, in truth, a corpse; only the hands above the surface. They tried to lift it; but it was impossible in all that muck. Being cross-questioned at length by Chavez, they thought, from the slenderness of the form, that it must be the body of a boy.

The man carrying the fishing pole lay it down almost reverentially upon the ground, looking at it and then sighing. Chavez said, "We'll call the constable's office and they will have to send out a dredger to remove the body. We can do no more for the poor lad now. He is far beyond our help I am afraid."

Lynton Viñas:
Shadow in the Darkness

Within hours, to the surprise of all, a dredger arrived to remove the body from the muck. A police inspector was there but neither the inspector nor anyone else could do anything until the remains were brought to shore, and it took the best part of the morning to accomplish that difficult operation. They had to sink no end of big stones in order to make a walkway across the mud. This done, the body was brought out. It proved to be the corpse of a boy of perhaps fourteen or fifteen years of age. There was a fracture ten centremetres long at the back of the skull, evidently fatal. This might, of course, have been an accidental injury; but when the body came to be raised from where it lay, it was found to be pinned down by a pitchfork, the handle of which had been afterwards whittled off, so as not to show above the water, a discovery tantamount to evidence of murder. The body was badly decomposed, which fretted Lynton even more, for she assumed it was the body of the shadow she had observed. Obviously

J. Wayne Frye

Lynton Viñas:
Shadow in the Darkness

it was not. So, her assumption that she had seen the boy's shadowy figure and then he was killed was erroneous for certain.

A crowd of witnesses came forward at this stage of the inquiry, stating that about a year ago, Mr. Benez, the school teacher, had staying with him a lad whom he called his nephew, and to whom it was supposed that he was not particularly kind. This lad was described as tall, thin, with long bony fingers. He generally wore clothing of the type corresponding in colour and texture to the shreds of clothing discovered on the body in the muck; and he was much addicted to fishing in the area where the body was found.

One thing led quickly to another. A local store identified the boy's sneakers as ones they carried. Other witnesses testified to angry scenes between the teacher and the boy whom he called his nephew. Finally, Benez gave himself up to

Lynton Viñas:
Shadow in the Darkness

authorities, confessed to the murder much to everyone's shock, and was immediately incarcerated in the local lockup while the police waited to move him to Manila.

And the motive for murder was freely admitted. The boy actually was not his nephew, but the teacher's own illegitimate son. The mother was dead, and the boy lived with his maternal grandmother in a remote part of Luzon. The old woman was poor, and Benez made her an annual allowance for looking after his son. He had not seen the boy for years, when he sent for him upon his grandmother's death. Perhaps he was weary of the tax upon his purse. Also, as he himself fully confessed, he was disappointed to find the boy despicable in intelligence and manners. He at all events took a dislike to the boy, which developed into positive hatred. The feeling of hatred was mutual, and the boy, being at the normal age for rebellion, in no uncertain terms made it plain he

J. Wayne Frye

Lynton Viñas:
Shadow in the Darkness

knew the teacher was his father and that he was going to tell the entire village.

Now, in a small village, the church still holds an inordinate sway over things, and the teacher, always acting like a devout Christian, was fearful that it would diminish his standing in the community. Add to that the fact the boy defied all discipline, was always off fishing, was wandering about the country side, and it was assumed by all that he was just there for a short visit, there was little concern when he was gone for almost a year.

At last there came a day when Benez had enough and followed him to the place where he fished. Benez admitted to simply deciding that he could no longer tolerate the boy, and catching up to him by the lake, beat him to death mercilessly. He weighted him down with rocks, braced him under the water with a broken pitchfork after tossing him in the lake, but apparently when the mine leaked the muck into the lake, it made the body rise. Still, Benez was baffled by how the fishing pole was in his hands as he had tossed it aside from the body. Oddly, Benez seemed to have little remorse for what he had done.

This is where the story gets really interesting. His dreadful secret had lately become intolerable for him. He was haunted by a shadowy figure that seemed to always be lurking about, always following him. He, himself, had taken to wearing a cloak at night, hoping that the shadowy figure would not recognize him.

. That presence appeared at many odd times and places, followed him in his walks, stood behind him in the school-room, and watched by his bedside. He only saw a shadow; but he knew who it was. He felt that his mind was becoming unravelled and that he was only holding onto sanity by a slender thread.

Lynton Viñas:
Shadow in the Darkness

Suffice it to say that Lynton completed her business in nearby Nangalisan in due time, but kept abreast of all the developments in regards to the case of the murdered boy, as her fascination with it preyed upon her mind. She had gone back to the village several times as she had even been included in the dedication ceremony for the new playground, which Father Mendez gratefully thanked her for as he informed her that it was her pleas to Mr. Chavez that had led him to finally donate the land. Truthfully, he had planned a donation all the time, but as will be seen later in the story, the Father's request was simply intended to get Lynton to spend time with Chavez. He had some unscrupulous plans intended for her.

There was never a trial, since it was assumed Benez had committed suicide. No particulars were ever given; just that he tied a sheet around his neck, tied the other end to the bars and ran furiously, snapping his neck.

Lynton Viñas:
Shadow in the Darkness

So ends this strange eventful history of Lynton's visit to Pittsfield or does it? You see, when she was visiting for the playground dedication something very unusual happened. During the dedication ceremonies, she noticed that strange shadow appearing around the corner of the church again. It was only for a split second, but it was there. However, it did not seem sinister. There appeared to be a peaceful countenance about it.

She mentioned it to Chavez, but again, he said that he saw nothing. Certain things she undoubtedly saw, she deduced, with her mind's eye, perhaps but she did see them just as I have described here; withholding nothing, adding nothing, explaining nothing more than can be explained. She resolved to put it out of her mind, but she could not stop asking herself, "Was it an illusion?"

CHAPTER 5

DYNAMIC DYNAMO GOES INTO ACTION

My imagination is fervently fed
Is the shadow something long dead
Is it a stranger or someone I knew
Oh, in the darkness give me my due

Should I scream at what I see
Or do I just let the shadow be
Is it just an illusion after all

J. Wayne Frye   91

Lynton Viñas:
Shadow in the Darkness

Yet I know what I saw

Shadows in darkness dance
And my sanity has no chance
Please help me I anxiously plead
For the shadow on my soul may feed

One might well think the tale would end here, as there could be no plausible explanation for what had apparently been the illusions experienced by Lynton. However, this is not the end, because what happened next is perhaps confirmation that we must all accept the fact that there are things that simply cannot and never will be adequately explained. Famed poet laureate, Lord Byron was one who knew that. Though he was an agnostic, he believed that something existed after death, not heaven or hell, but some astral plain where lost souls with unfinished business in life went to wander, trying desperately to come back to finish the unfinished.

J. Wayne Frye

Lynton Viñas:
Shadow in the Darkness

It has been wisely said, that one fool makes many; and it hath been poetically observed by a Pope of the Catholic Church that fools rush in where angels fear to tread. Thus, do the church and the religious often tarry in trepidation and fear while so called fools rush in to confront the injustice and despicable that others recoil from. Now, I would never call Lynton a fool, as she is a woman of intricate delicacies who always thoroughly assesses a situation before jumping into the fray. However, in this instance, she was about to witness another occurrence that would solidify her reasoning that she had not seen illusions, and that what she saw was a plea, a beckoning spirit that simply was not and could not rest until someone righted a horrible wrong.

If Lynton had not rushed in where she had no business, none of this would have been written. It is impossible that I am not making a mountain out of a molehill, but the sometimes dull

Lynton Viñas:
Shadow in the Darkness

impudence and impious nature of the author of this book cannot belie the fact that I lay before you what is, without any doubt, my most humble affirmation of what Lord Byron laid out for us all in his epic ghost poem long ago.

Be aware that what follows is compiled from the source herself, Lynton Viñas, as reliable, honest, kind, caring, justice-committed person as ever drew breath on this place called earth. Though some will decry this as blasphemous indictment and even seditious acrimoniousness in the minds of many, those people may be damned as far as this author is concerned, for I lay before you what I know as truth, because it comes from the most truthful and reliable person I have ever known.

With regard to the supernatural personages treated herein, I can only say that I am an eternal sceptic, but offer my heartfelt belief in the integrity of Lynton Viñas. It is possible that some

Lynton Viñas:
Shadow in the Darkness

readers may object, in these objectionable times, to the freedom with which saints, angels and spiritual persons discourse in this vision, but, for precedents upon such points, I must refer the reader to Fielding's *Journey from this World to the Next*. I know not if there is another life or not. Frankly, I seriously doubt it as I put what I consider fairy tales behind me long ago, but I am relating a tale, not passing judgement on it. What happened I believe happened, because I believe in Lynton Viñas.

Lynton left the dedication ceremony that day, declining Chavez's invitation to go back to his estate, because frankly, she knew that she would have to, as she had so frequently of late, fight off his amorous advances. She crossed the same path she had wandered onto way back when the whole affair concerning illusions had started. As she made her way past the school, she felt uneasiness. Someone was following her. She turned, looked

Lynton Viñas:
Shadow in the Darkness

back into the gathering fog, but no one was there. When she turned back, there in the distance maybe no more than 20 feet was that old shadowy apparition of a young boy, no doubt, obviously carrying a fishing pole.

This time, there was sound emanating from the shadow. It was low, sorrowful and pleading. There were no words, just tearful sounds that seemed to bore into Lynton's consciousness and penetrate her soul. The figure was so dark that it stood out even though it was in the dark shadows of the overhanging banana trees that darkened the whole area.

Lynton did not move. She was mesmerized now by the apparition. It was not disappearing this time. It seemed determined to communicate somehow with her. She stood perfectly still, and summoning all her courage she said, "What is it you want of me?"

Lynton Viñas:
Shadow in the Darkness

The apparition did not reply, just kept weeping until it suddenly pointed to its left toward a path winding through a clump of banana trees. The left arm of the apparition stayed extended as the weeping continued. It kept pointing and mournfully sighing. Then, it moved onto the path, walking down it until it disappeared into the darkness.

It was obvious that the apparition had something to show Lynton, something that was somewhere among the clump of trees. Without fear or hesitation, the woman who would one day be hailed as the dynamic dynamo demon fighter, moved steadily and cautiously into the banana grove. The path was winding and hard to follow, but she would not tarry in her determination to finally get to the bottom of what these ghostly apparitions were all about. She decided that all along, this thing – whatever it was, wanted to share some dark secret with her.

Lynton Viñas:
Shadow in the Darkness

She trudged on for what seemed like hours, but in fact, was maybe five or six minutes. The sun was slowly going down in a cold pale flare of light. The trees grew dark. The undulating shadows leaned to the east as she came to a small clearing and there it was, a stark looking old stone two story house, seemingly abandoned. As she stood staring, she heard the lonely call of a lone bird in the distance, moaning, squawking as if in pain. She looked up at a second floor window and there it was – the dark shadow standing in front of a window, beckoning to her.

Pale slate-grey clouds whirled up around the now rising moon. There she stood staring at the beckoning one, as if she were the inquisitive dreamer of dreams, the eternal asker of questions in the chilly night air of discontent. Purple hues seemed to swirl around the house, and still the shadowy figure just kept beckoning, almost pleading with her to come in.

J. Wayne Frye

Lynton Viñas:
Shadow in the Darkness

Here, what started Chapter 1 bears repeating:

Go to the gate, sweet Lynton and do not fall

There where the vines cling crimson on the wall,

And in the twilight wait for what will come.

The leaves will whisper there of death, and some,

Like flying words, will strike you as they fall;

But go, and if you listen, evil will call.

Go to the dark gate, sweet Lynton and be brave,

For the you have souls to save.

No, there is not a dawn in eastern skies

To rift the fiery night that's in lurking eyes;

But there, where western glooms are gathering

The dark will pour upon the dark, if anything:

Good slays itself with every leaf that flies,

And hell is more than half of paradise.

No, there is not a dawn in eastern skies -

In those distant eastern skies.

Out of a grave he comes to tell you this,

Lynton Viñas:
Shadow in the Darkness

Out of a grave he comes to quench the kiss

That flames upon your forehead with a glow,

That blinds you to the way that you must go.

Yes, there is yet one way to where he is,

Bitter, but one that faith may never miss.

Out of a grave he comes to tell you this—

To tell you this.

There is the dark gate, do not fall,

There are the crimson leaves upon the wall,

Go, for the winds are tearing them away,

Nor think to riddle the dead words they say,

Nor any more to feel them as they fall;

But go, and trust not evil's call.

There by the dark gate, do not fall,

For evil's search will not stall.

She was about to seek the faces of truth within,
for she knew though danger might lie ahead there
were answers to the unanswerable awaiting her.
There seemed to be quiet whispers on the now

J. Wayne Frye

Lynton Viñas:
Shadow in the Darkness

slight breeze, whispers that were urging her into the old abandoned house.

The eternal asker of answers becomes as the darkness on a wind blown over a myriad forest, and the truth dances as nymphs in tropical rain. Still, he beckoned, and she knew he could not be denied, because within was the truth of a mystery she did not even know existed.

There was now a symphony playing in her head as the wind picked up. The wind was music she had heard somewhere before. She looked up and the shadow was gone, but her curiosity had not disappeared. With trepidation but determination, she opened the creaky door, walked into the foyer and with steadiness ascended the staircase and all the while she felt the emptiness of the house begin to overwhelm her. It was not just a physical emptiness; it was an emptiness of the soul. This was a place of evil.

Lynton Viñas:
Shadow in the Darkness

All humanity is burdened with a dearth of hope in a world where greed rules like an ancient sovereign with complete control. Yet, this was more than the evil of greed that had, like the capitalist monster unleashed by the rule of Ronald Reagan and Margaret Thatcher, devoured the world and strangled hope for so many years, this was evil of a different kind, evil that fed on itself and like the barons of greed on Wall Street, knew no way to be satisfied. Like a capitalist wanting more and more, whatever evil abounded in this abominable house was insatiable. It had to feed on evil. You could feel evil breathing in the walls, hanging from the chandeliers, pulsating under the carpets, vibrating with delight in the darkness that engulfed Lynton now, seeming to chill her with its insidiousness.

Within these walls a supreme evil had dwelt. She could feel it. Those who perpetrated the evil were gone, but, oh my, the evil had an afterglow

Lynton Viñas:
Shadow in the Darkness

that bathed this horror house in a malignancy that could never be excised. You simply could not cut out the evil that had abounded here. It was as permanent as America's love of guns.

As Lynton neared the landing at the top of the stairs, in front of her, down a long hallway was the dark shadowy figure, motioning her toward a room on her right. There was a mist down the hallway as Lynton peered toward the door on her right, where the shadow still pointed. It was as if she was in a dream as she slowly moved toward the room, where she assumed danger lurked. Wave after wave of horror shattered all about Lynton. Still, she slowly moved toward the door. She blinked, and the shadow was gone, but her need to see what was behind the door had not diminished at all.

She looked down the hallway. The walls were painted black, and there were many pentagrams in

Lynton Viñas:
Shadow in the Darkness

orderly fashion nailed to the walls, clinging like luminous birds to the sides of cliffs, glistening in the darkness and seeming to vibrate. Each one seemed to be glaring at her like a golden eye. And behind them all the ghosts of thoughts went moving, restlessly moving as if there were souls trapped in the walls.

Lynton was one who had known no fear, for she faced danger head on, but this night she felt fear in her bones as if stones would freeze in her veins. She lost herself in the moment and seemed to hear murmuring voices and shuffling feet.

We are all born of flesh, in a flare of pain, and long forget the red roots from whence we rose, but we know that we rose and walked, and that after a while we shall lie down again, embracing death. It was here, all around this hallway, death as pronounced as Lynton had ever experienced. But it was hideous death, vile death, evil death.

J. Wayne Frye

Lynton Viñas:
Shadow in the Darkness

Finally, at the door, she gripped the handle and turned it slowly. She took a deep breath and prepared to face evil. Slowly opening the door, the moonlight shone through the window, bathing the room in a subdued light. The room was mostly empty. There was nothing frightening about it at all. An old worn out chair was in the far corner, and a strange looking long flat cabinet maybe three feet high was over by the window. Looking down at the carpeted floor, it appeared the cabinet had been pushed over by the window as there were indentations on the carpet indicating the cabinet had been pushed across it.

Lynton ambled about the room in a nonchalant fashion. She walked over to the window and noticed the moon basking the top of the cabinet in an eerie glow. The cabinet was maybe 6 feet in length and three to four feet wide. Something seemed to compel her to reach under the overhang at the top of the cabinet. Then, the shock hit her.

Lynton Viñas:
Shadow in the Darkness

There was a leather rope with steel inserts attaching it under the table top. She walked to the end of the table top, placed her hand under the overhang and there was another leather rope. She ran her right hand across the wooden top and there were pits and groves, obviously made by a knife.

The realization hit upon her instantly as she looked around the room. This was a place where Satanists were meeting, and could this table of horrors be used for sacrifices? Surely, they had only sacrificed animals she thought as she looked over at the far wall and noticed that the carpet was not tacked under the baseboards. It was just rolled out onto the floor beneath. She walked over to the far wall, bent down, lifted the carpet and began to roll it up, exposing a wooden floor, but she also exposed something more as she got toward the middle of the room. Although she stopped, because the cabinet was preventing her from rolling any more of the carpet, what she saw was a

J. Wayne Frye

Lynton Viñas:
Shadow in the Darkness

manifestation of evil. There, on the floor was a huge pentagram. There was no doubt in her mind now. Satanists were at play in the small village of Pittsfield and had made a human sacrifice.

She carefully rolled the carpet back out, surveyed the room as she was preparing to leave and at the door noticed something caught on a rough edge where the door latch was embedded in the door jam. It was a very tiny piece of black cloth. Obviously, someone had caught his or her pants, skirt, whatever, on the rough edge and torn some material off. She reached down and removed the maybe 2 centremetre by 2 centremetre piece of cloth. She placed the tiny piece of material in her blouse pocket and headed out of the room.

Down long broad flights of dark stairs she gracefully and quietly flowed. The quiet was almost deafening, scattered as in waves on some far and distant shore.

Lynton Viñas:
Shadow in the Darkness

As she reached the bottom of the stairs, her emotions were broken into small cascades of wonderment as she looked back up at the landing. Then, above her in the intense darkness at the top of the stairs was the shadowy figure. There was a gleaming stab of sadness, vague and incoherent, something dreamlike about the figure that stood there, penetrating dark eyes she noticed for the first time. Yes, they were sad and pleading for something from her. There were whispers of pain in the eyes, a cry for help. No, there was a cry for justice!

At that very moment, a revelation swept over Lynton like the foaming waves of a white-lined shivering sea. She looked directly into those pleading eyes and with determination said, "I shall not fail you as I seek justice and put my weary hands on the banisters of retribution against those who defiled you. I know who you are, and I know you were not killed at the lake."

J. Wayne Frye

Lynton Viñas:
Shadow in the Darkness

Lynton knew that Mr. Benez had not committed suicide. She knew that his so-called nephew had not been killed at the lake, but rather, had been sacrificed to Satan right there in that abominable house of evil.

The fisherman draws his streaming net from the sea and sails toward the far shore. The dark bow plunges up and down in the foaming blue-black waves, and the shrill rain seethes like ghostly music about him in a quiet shower of discontent that the shoreline is but a dream and that he will not make it there. Lynton could sense the rain shrilly singing on the lapsing waves of despair. Like a shadow of shifting silver it danced to the tune of death. Yet, she had no fear. Rather, she was filling with righteous indignation as she looked up at the top of the stairs and the shadow had once again disappeared, but the wrath of this woman had not disappeared. She was ready to do battle now.

Lynton Viñas:
Shadow in the Darkness

She walked out of the house, closing the door behind her furiously, as she seethed with anger that killers were on the loose in the tiny village of Pittsfield. The dynamic dynamo was about to go into action.

CHAPTER 6

THE SCALE OF JUSTICE

There is a ghost of singing fury.
An elfin voice blowing about,
Weaving to a babble of sound,
Crying in the dark a secret.

Lynton stands bold and strong
By he who was so unjustly defiled.
She is the one who feels your pain.

J. Wayne Frye   111

Lynton Viñas:
Shadow in the Darkness

The bell of redemption is about to toll.

She goes about in quiet determination
Not invisible to your pain.
She stands by your side
Though your life is dim and low.

Though tempests sweep by her,
She can see through the dark night.
She is as waves on a midnight sea
And is calm and resolute.

Lynton spent the night at the inn and dreamed of darkness, broken music and broken hope. She dreamed that she walked beneath high trees and the sun shined brightly down as she saw that young boy in the distance. She moved toward him and was preparing to kiss his face, when a furious wind came and caught him up in it. She woke up in a sweat as she saw the crashing of boulders flung down from above the trees.

J. Wayne Frye

Lynton Viñas:
Shadow in the Darkness

She was reminded of how darkness can fall so quickly sometimes, unexpected, as it had fallen upon the poor lad who was sacrificed to a fairy tale. There was no heaven, and the only hell was right here and right now on earth. People endured the hell of want in a world of plenty. There were no little red men running around with pitch forks poking people for eternity who had sinned. There were devils aplenty though walking among the living. They were the barons of greed whose insatiable desire for more and more trapped the many in slavery to the few. Call it what you wanted, the modern world of corporate capitalism was a living hell for 99% of the people. Most were like drowning souls going down for the third time and there was no lifeguard in the world of greed to help. Everyone knew that eventually they would sink into the grime and stench that wrapped itself around you and pulled you under. This was the modern world, but it was a world to which Lynton Viñas, dynamic dynamo, would not succumb.

Lynton Viñas:
Shadow in the Darkness

She rose, paced the floor waiting for the sun to come up. She read an old newspaper for a few minutes as she eased back in an overstuffed chair. She folded the paper back up and turned away. She thought back over what she had seen and the knowledge she had accumulated.

Some people hear alarm bells but just sit and listen. The cold light of the truth had slapped her in the face. She looked out the window and the rain was pouring down in waves and ripples that beaded up on the window. Life itself was buried in rain she thought, buried by misery caused by those who preyed upon the unsuspecting. For most, life is shrewdly betrayed as misfortunate bites at their heels. So many in the world cry and they are not heard.

The wind hurled and pounded against the window. There was a torrent pouring out from the heavens. She thought of the shadow's pain.

J. Wayne Frye

Lynton Viñas:
Shadow in the Darkness

Wind; wind; wind; carving the walls of the inn with fury, water gleaming in the streets for the country has no infrastructure to contain nature, as it might make the rich pay their fair share. She gazed out into the darkness and down the nearby dark alley an old tree cracked and fell. Trees limbs waved back and forth in the haunted air. The darkness was whistling a tune.

She could not get the vision of the suffering poor lad out of her mind. The wind was shrieking. The wind was grieving. The tumult and furious wind howled as if uttering his pain.

Then, as suddenly as it started it ended. The quivering wind did not die down. It just stopped as if someone had snapped their fingers and said "quit." The dark empty pallor of the night dissipated and dawn burst forth. Lynton walked about the room and deep within she vowed that justice would be done.

J. Wayne Frye   115

Lynton Viñas:
Shadow in the Darkness

She dressed with determination as the white fog crept from the nearby sea over the village and over the pale grey dilapidated hovels that people called home, except, of course, for the stately mansion at the end of the street where all wealth lay in the hands of one man named Chavez.

Along damp sinuous streets, the fog crawled as if it was harbouring evil within its midst. It curled like a dream among the now motionless trees as the humidity began to climb and the streets came to life with those who had to hustle for their daily rice. While the church encouraged people to be fruitful and multiply, it did nothing to assure those who were born had food, shelter, healthcare, education, a job. The fog was like an omen of more poverty, more despair in a land where few had any hope. The fog was the haze of misery that gripped people in its grasp and squeezed and squeezed until there was nothing else left to squeeze out of them.

J. Wayne Frye

Lynton Viñas:
Shadow in the Darkness

Lynton, dressed now, from the window looked down at the village covered in the fog, and thought to herself that perhaps this was all just a dream and that she would soon awaken from the darkness that had held her in its grip for so long now.

She sighed and prepared to face the reality of what she must do. First, she would go to the town lock-up and talk with the jailer to get as much information as possible on Benez's suicide.

Walking to the jail, the city was now awakening in full force as the streets clogged with belching vehicles spewing the poison of commerce as people rubbed the darkness from their eyes while they gazed like zombies at another fruitless day in the land of want. They all had sombre eyes, because their secret fears were vaguely unfolding for yet another day scurrying for survival. There is no seed of hope to be planted, for the harvest barely produces enough for sustenance.

Lynton Viñas:
Shadow in the Darkness

Each gleaming point of light is like a seed that dilates into nothingness. Each cloud becomes a rapidly dimming face, and each hurrying face has that blank stare of hopelessness. This is the world of the poor. Ah, and the lad who was murdered was poor, so he was just another meaningless person in the endless sea of humanity.

The jail was at the middle of town with vacant lots on each side of it that were covered with piles of debris discarded by people who had no idea of sanitation. Disease flourished among the poor, because they received none of the good things reserved for the wealthy. Why did they need sanitation, they were but cogs in the giant wheel of commerce. They were the expendable who worked for a few pesos a day so that those at the top of the economic ladder might have lives of luxurious splendour. This was the way of a world where there was no compassion, no heart and no concern for those at the bottom.

J. Wayne Frye

Lynton Viñas:
Shadow in the Darkness

Now, this tale I am spinning took place many years ago, so Lynton's beauty had not matured yet, but still she cut a dashingly fine figure that caught all men's attention. The jailer was quick to rise and greet her with a broad smile. "My, it is Lynton Viñas. I know you, and what may I do for you this fine morning?"

As he handed her a cup of coffee, she gladly accepted as she said, "I want to talk to you about Mr. Benez and his suicide."

"Not much to discuss. I found him early in the morning. He simply tied one end of a sheet to one of the bars, and obviously ran as hard as he could, snapping his neck."

Lynton, placing her coffee cup on the table, leaned forward and said, "OK, but can you tell me if he was acting despondent, indicating that he might be contemplating doing himself in?"

"Not particularly. He seemed fairly normal for a guy facing a murder charge that is. He obviously was not very jovial."

"Did he have any visitors beforehand?"

The jailer took a deep breath, and though he seemed reluctant, he stuttered out several names. "There was Father Mendez, Robert Chavez who came by with his friend Blackman Perez, and, of course, the inn keeper, Mr. Sanchez, who brings over all the prisoners' meals.

"And did they indicate why they wanted to see him?"

"No, they did not, but it is normal for Father Mendez to visit the prisoners. He does it often as part of his duties I suppose, but, of course, he was well-acquainted with Mr. Benez. One might even say they were friends. Had been for years. Mr.

Lynton Viñas:
Shadow in the Darkness

Chavez and Mr. Perez said they wanted to try and explore the reasons why he would have killed the boy as they felt he might be hiding something. I saw no reason to deny them access. After all, Mr. Chavez is our most prominent citizen."

"And how long after these visits did he die?"

The jailer picked up a thick notebook, flipped backward through it, handed it to Lynton as he said, "There you are, the times they went in are all there."

Looking down at the page, Lynton noticed the following:

NAME	TIME IN	TIME OUT
R. Sanchez	7:30 AM	7:35 AM
R. Sanchez	12:00 AM	12:05 PM
R. Sanchez	6:00 PM	6:10 PM
Father Mendez	6:30 PM	6:40 PM
R. Chavez & B. Perez	6:50 PM	7:00 PM

Lynton Viñas:
Shadow in the Darkness

"And you accompanied them back to the cell?"

Pointing at the door behind him, he replied, "No, there was no need. That door is unlocked. They simply let themselves into the cellblock, and walked down the hallway to his cell at the very back."

Lynton quizzically asked, "Were there any other prisoners at the time?"

"Oh no, we rarely have more than one prisoner at a time. Most of the time, like today, we have none."

"And what time was Mr. Benez found dead?"

"It was around 6:00 AM that I discovered him."

"And the coroner estimated the time of death as what?"

Lynton Viñas:
Shadow in the Darkness

"Between 6 and 8?"

Lynton noticed some keys hanging on the side of the desk, actually out of sight of the jailer. She assumed they were to the cells. Wondering if it was possible to take them without him noticing, she smiled at him, reached down and grasped them. He did not take any notice of her touching the keys. She said, "Could I look at the cell where he was?"

"Sure, no problem," he replied as he reached down to the side of the desk and picked up the keys.

They walked back to the cell, and Lynton asked if she could go in. She then asked if she could remove the sheet from the bunk, and she did. She tied one end around the bar and then stretched it out. "Possible," she uttered as she thought to herself that he could have snapped his own neck.

J. Wayne Frye   123

Lynton Viñas:
Shadow in the Darkness

She looked up at the ceiling and there were two small beams running perpendicular to one another cross ways in the cell. She looked over at the bunk bed, and it was under one of the beams. She walked over, looked down at the concrete floor and saw scratch marks on it, as if the bed had been moved.

The jailer was looking intently at her as she said, "Has the bed been moved at all?"

"No, it is exactly where it was when he was found."

"Were there any marks on the body other than round the neck?

"There was a large bump on his head, but the coroner assumed it was from the fall after he snapped his neck. It was a rather large welt on his left temple."

Lynton Viñas:
Shadow in the Darkness

"Thank you," said Lynton as she exited the cell, convinced that Benez, like the young boy, had been murdered, and there were four prime suspects that she had in mind, as they all had access to the prisoner. She thanked the jailer for his cooperation, and bid him good day. As she stepped out the front door, she heard the jailer frantically pounding the keys on the phone, obviously calling someone. She stood by the door and heard him whisper, "She was here. She suspects something."

Puddles of water flashed in the sun and a skinny old black cat meandering down the sidewalk seemed to wink green amber eyes at her. The butcher stood by his window tying his apron; others scurried about opening their businesses. She lowered her eyes to gaze at the sidewalk, as she walked slowly toward the Chavez mansion. Her thoughts were blown and scattered like the leaves fluttering about in the morning breeze. As

Lynton Viñas:
Shadow in the Darkness

she wiggled down the street men gawked and women smiled, but she was in deep thought and did not notice or care. She was on the trail of a murderer, and now, although Benez had admitted it, she knew that he did not kill the young boy either. But why would he be willing to admit a crime he did not commit?

She felt her body seem to float down the street as she was in deep thought. Her brain was now like a vapour in the morning mist. The trees about her were exhaling the ghosts of the late night rain. People were talking, laughing, as if things were alright, but they did not know there was a murderer at large in their midst.

Like notes in a soft melody, people bear their misery in solitude, hoping for the light, but knowing there will probably only be darkness. The wanderer of hope dreams of happiness, and smiles at the hostile sky, but as the people of the village

J. Wayne Frye

Lynton Viñas:
Shadow in the Darkness

went about their business, they had no idea that there was insidious evil all about them. Or did they? Were some of them embracing the evil, too?

She walked past a woman sitting in front of a fortune telling parlour who said as she extended her right hand with cards in it. "Draw three cards. I will tell your future. Draw three cards, and lay them down, rest your palms upon them, stare at me and think of nothing, nothing at all. Look into my eyes as they are like a curtain to the future and they will slowly draw open tomorrow for you."

Lynton was as if in a trance. She had no faith in fortune tellers, but she let the old lady go on. The woman said, "Upon a scarlet cloth a white skull lies. Your hand is on the hand that holds three lilies. You will live long, if you do not pressure fate. I see a dark person here who will betray you. I see a shadow of secret crimes. There are those who smiled at you while they lied. There is a

Lynton Viñas:
Shadow in the Darkness

ghost of murder in your blood, coming or past, I do not know which. I see a dark shadow in your future or maybe it is in your past, or maybe it is both."

Lynton laid a 50 peso bill on the table and smiled. She turned to walk away, and heard the lady texting frantically on her cell phone. Lynton thought perhaps the whole town was a pack of Satanists and they were all part of great conspiracy.

She felt that she was in deathly peril as she ambled forlornly down the street. Round white clouds rolled slowly above the housetops. Over mostly tin roofs the clouds flowed gently and softly, moving ever so slowly toward the mountaintop in the far distance. A flock of birds rose with wings flashing and a little boy passed by her whistling a familiar tune, but she could not remember its name.

Lynton Viñas:
Shadow in the Darkness

Two young lovers were sitting by the fountain holding hands and looking longingly into each others eyes, but when they noticed Lynton, they looked up with piercing eyes, seeming to glare at her. Was she now becoming paranoid? She suddenly felt as if all eyes were on her. She was used to being stared at, but not this way.

The light wind blew in her ears a sound of muted laughter, as youths shuffled by on their way to school. One boy laughed as he passed. Was he laughing at her?

Ah, but there was a clearer sound Lynton was hearing in her head. Yet, it was more in her heart than in her ears. Her heart was pounding now like a hammer driving a nail as she looked up at the Chavez mansion that spoke of the great divide that separated the rich and poor, a divide that grew greater every day as governments handed those at the top more and more while ignoring the poor.

Lynton Viñas:
Shadow in the Darkness

There was a melody playing in Lynton's head now, playing with delicate strokes that sombre scale that she embraced with gusto – the scale of justice!

Lynton Viñas:
Shadow in the Darkness

CHAPTER 7

THE ONE AND ONLY DYNAMIC DYNAMO

Is time but a dream within a dream
Or is it a nightmare within a nightmare
Time lays great cities in dust
Time covers the face of beauty
Time tumbles walls
Time can strangle love
Time can burn hope like fire
Time turns dreams grey and devours them

J. Wayne Frye

Lynton Viñas:
Shadow in the Darkness

Ah, but what of the shadows in darkness
What does time do to them
Time embraces death as a friend
Time to death is never an ending
Time to death is a never changing
Time to death is beautiful
Time is death in one dream flowing into another
Time is death in symphonic transition
Time is death embraced and fondled

Lynton stood at the gate and looked up at the study window and saw sitting in the morning light the master of the estate. He was reading a book. She could faintly make out the sunlight touching his left hand as he thumbed a page. He was, indeed, an incredibly handsome man. Maybe she and been remiss all those years spurning his advances she thought.

She sauntered through the gate, and proceeded toward the front door. She rang the bell and the

J. Wayne Frye

butler greeted her cheerfully, not suggesting she be announced. He simply pointed to the top of the stairs and said, "He is in the study, first door to your right.

As she walked in, Chavez rose quickly, as did his friend on his right – Blackman Perez. They both seemed thrilled to see her, but she wondered if it was perhaps all an act.

Smiling broadly, Blackman said, "What a pleasant surprise to be able to look upon a thing of such beauty this early in the day."

Robert interjected, "Indeed, you always bring a bright light of loveliness wherever you go."

"Watch it boys, you may give me a swelled head."

Pointing at a nearby chair, indicating she should

Lynton Viñas:
Shadow in the Darkness

take a seat, Robert Chavez said, "And what may I ask brings you to my humble abode?"

Lynton wanted dramatic effect, so she simply said, "Murder!"

The two men were obviously shocked by her abruptness. Lynton continued. "You both know the boy was killed, because Benez admitted to it, but he did not commit the crime, nor did he commit suicide."

Their shock was subsiding, but not their dismay at Lynton's abrupt nature. Robert said, "So, you have uncovered some evidence to prove these allegations."

"Perhaps," replied Lynton with assuredness. "I have been to an old abandoned house off the path between here and Nangalisan. What I found indicates that Satanists are here about."

Lynton Viñas:
Shadow in the Darkness

Laughing, Blackman said, "Satanists? My Lynton, I think you are letting your imagination run a bit wild."

"I saw a sacrificial altar. I saw pentagrams. I also have evidence, and believe me, Benez did not commit suicide. He was silenced because of what he knew."

Blackman arose and walked about the room as he said, "Then why would he confess to a murder he did not commit. It does not make sense."

"Oh, it makes perfect sense if you believe your confederates will get you out, and probably reward you because you are covering up a big conspiracy of silence in regards to Satanism in this village."

Robert was shaking his head as he said, "Nonsense, absolute nonsense, there is no proof. The house was probably used by kids for games."

Lynton Viñas:
Shadow in the Darkness

"Then these kids are playing some serious games."

Blackman walked over to where she was sitting. "O.K., take us to this house. Let is examine it for evidence of these Satanists you think are plying their trade here."

They took Blackman's car and parked on the periphery of the forested area. The afternoon had crept up on them and the heat was oppressive, but as Lynton made her way with them to the house, the trees were in bloom, blossoms falling and the birds were singing. The trek was not long but the heat made it seem farther than it was.

They did not hesitate to walk in, and it appeared that the two men were familiar with the place, as she had not told them where the room that concerned her was. Yet, they bounded up the stairs and went right to it.

Lynton Viñas:
Shadow in the Darkness

The room was empty. The cabinet and chair were gone. The two men look quizzically at her as she walked over to the carpet, rolled it back to show them the pentagram. It was gone too.

Blackman said, "And you are sure this is the room?"

The silence between them flowed past like dividing waters. Dreamlike they stood. Lynton breathed the fragrance of doubt with permeated the room. Time dissolved into shrugging shoulders by the two men. Clouds had formed outside and lightning sparkled in the distance with a long quiver of light that glistened in the sky. Lynton spoke softly, as she sank into waves of contemplation. "They were here. Obviously, someone decided to get rid of all the evidence."

Robert took a deep breath and said, "Perhaps. You are sure this is the right house?"

Lynton Viñas:
Shadow in the Darkness

Lynton did not like his condescending tone, but she elected to ignore it. She reached into her blouse pocket where she had put the one shred of evidence that might connect someone to the house. She did not bring it out, electing to keep it to herself.

She sank in waves of quiet; she seemed to float in a sea of silence as she collected her thoughts. "Well, let us walk back to the car. Obviously, this place has been scrubbed clean of any evidence."

At the bottom of the stairs, Blackman placed his hand on Lynton's shoulder, looked at her with intensity, smiled and said, "It's OK kid. I believe you."

Robert said nothing. They left the house and walked in a light rain to the car. On the way back to Robert's place, Lynton kept reflecting on the evidence she had gathered. It was damning.

J. Wayne Frye

Lynton Viñas:
Shadow in the Darkness

The evening was spent in meaningless conversation about mundane things, as if the two men did not want to discuss the whole sordid affair evolving around what Lynton had seen. She excused herself for the night, and despite Robert's plea to stay, she went back to the inn.

The night was humid as usual, and as she moved down the quiet, deserted street, she felt that there was something menacing about in the darkness. She could not see a presence, but she felt it. Walls of fright trap many people, and Lynton had known fear before, but she always faced it head on. Walls of fear keep people incarcerated atom by atom in a prison of the mind. This was a woman born of fire and ice who could rage against the storm like a blazing fire, and if push came to shove, she was like cold, impenetrable ice that could freeze the fingers of fright that bind most people in a cocoon they use to ward off a world they cannot understand.

Lynton Viñas:
Shadow in the Darkness

She heard the faint sound of footsteps behind her to the left. She took a big breath of night air. One can face danger, but sometimes one must run from it in order to gain advantage. Death lurks among us and it is often silent, but this night she heard the faint sound of death behind her. This was not her imagination. Something sinister was there in the dark.

Someone had died horribly on that table on top of the cabinet. The broken body had been tossed into the lake by a party or parties as yet unknown, though her suspicions were forming. She was the next victim, because, though she was still unsure of what she actually knew, the killer or killers did not know that. Her breasts rose and fell precipitously, her breath quivered. The faint footsteps were getting closer. Did she dare turn and face the assumed assailant as she was a woman of some boxing skill, developed in hard gym work over the years.

Lynton Viñas:
Shadow in the Darkness

Fighting for breath; her cheeks were flushed to scarlet, and suddenly she whirled around to face whatever was there. She shouted, "Show yourself fiend. I'll kick your ass from here to Manila!"

Fury hurried along through her veins as she stared into the darkness behind her. There was nothing but silence. Then she saw it. In an alley to her right, a long silver blade flashed in the moonlight. A figure, head covered by a hooded jacket, suddenly sprang out, knife extended in right hand as he ran frantically toward her, ready to penetrate the soft flesh of the dynamic dynamo.

Thoughts flashed in her mind of the momentous decision to journey here on her trip to Nangalisan. Had she never ventured here, none of this would have happened, but then again, murderers would have avoided detection, too. Backward dreams were not her forte, as she always looked forward, not backward, so she was happy with her choice.

Lynton Viñas:
Shadow in the Darkness

The knife was glistening in the moonlight, speaking in silence of death in its gleaming evil. She could have run, but her high heels were no match for a fleet footed assailant. So, she stood her ground despite rhythmic feet that may have been able to outrun the assailant barefooted.

She waited for his lunge with confidence. When he made it, she parried with her right hand, striking his right inside forearm, deflecting the knife to her right. She then rammed her knee into his groin and he dropped the knife as he crumbled to the ground in excruciating pain. Just as she was about to deliver the coup-de-grâce with a final ramming of her high heel into his crotch, he rolled over, scrambled to his feet and ran quickly back down the street. She elected not to pursue him as she decided discretion was the better part of valour. She took a deep breath, reached down and picked up the knife. Look out evil ones when you go up against the one and only dynamic dynamo!

J. Wayne Frye

Lynton Viñas:
Shadow in the Darkness

CHAPTER 8

THEY EMBRACED AND KISSED

Dance to the left,
Dance to the right.
It is fight, fight, fight.
Dynamic dynamo-trick up sleeve.

She fights a nightmare,
In a world of fright,
With all her might.
Dynamic dynamo-trick up sleeve.

She fights for the truth.
She fights against lies,

J. Wayne Frye

Lynton Viñas:
Shadow in the Darkness

As convention she defies
Dynamic dynamo-trick up sleeve.

This is the girl who fights demons,
With verve and determined intensity.
Left hook has a meteor's velocity.
Dynamic dynamo-trick up sleeve.

Sometimes facing danger and overcoming it pumps adrenalin through your body like a raging river through a gorge. Lynton was exhilarated, because she had confronted evil head on and delivered a blow for justice. She lifted her face to the light of the moon and a feeling of self-satisfaction danced in her head. Her dress was purple, her high heels were golden, her eyes were dark and penetrating; and a bright rose of pride opened its heart in her pounding breast. She turned and walked up the street, knife in hand, prancing to the surly languor of the rhythmic music of victory. She had floored opponents in the boxing ring, where she excelled as a pugilistic wonder, but no victory felt better than this one.

J. Wayne Frye

Lynton Viñas:
Shadow in the Darkness

The violins were weaving a weft of silver chords. The horns were weaving a lustrous blend of golden melodies and time was caught in a glistening pattern that made her proud and determined. She was alive, really alive!

Shadows of assuredness fell over her face, and she knew she would never bow before evil. Every step she took was a step toward the sunlight of truth which would shine on the darkness that had engulfed the little village.

Death, which at first had thought of her as easy prey when the knife was brandished, was sulking now in discontent, because it had met a fighter. She was a murderer too, a murderer of complacency. Always, in her dreams, she had met adversity and won, and now as she aged, adversity was snapping at many people's heels day in and day out who had not the courage to fight. That is when the dynamic dynamo stood up for them.

Lynton Viñas:
Shadow in the Darkness

She was about 50 feet from the inn when she sensed someone or something staring at her off to her right. She turned, knowing instinctively what was there, half-dreading but also half delighted at what she expected to see. The shadow lurked there in an alleyway, piercing eyes red with fire. Was it there or was it just in her mind? The shadow lifted its right hand, made a waving motion and the fire in the eyes turned calm and serene. Whatever it was, there was no malevolence toward Lynton. It was pleased with her.

She walked through the inn lobby and bar, with a determined stride, head held high, carrying the knife. The patrons stared in disbelief and the innkeeper, Richard Sanchez, sweating profusely and breathing heavily, followed her intently with his eyes. She looked over at him, smiled and said flippantly, as she looked down at the knife, "For cutting up Satanists who want to mess with a little Filipino girl."

Lynton Viñas:
Shadow in the Darkness

She took a shower, combed her silky long black hair as she looked out the window into the darkness. Leaves fluttered past her window, and she thought of graves being dug in the earth, and coffins that passed in a parade toward darkness. Evil was lurking all about and she had met it head-on that night. She came out triumphant, but two others had not been so lucky.

She called down and asked for three newspapers. Though she had not met him yet, she had read Wayne Frye's books, and remembered how his famous private eye, Aaron Adams, often slept at night to make sure he was ready for any culprits who might try to do him in. She spread the newspapers all around the bed, turned out the lights, placed the knife under her pillow and drifted off into a peaceful slumber thinking of the man she desired to bring her love and devotion. She dreamed of what Wayne Frye had once written about love. It soothed her troubled mind to

Lynton Viñas:
Shadow in the Darkness

reflect on his words. *Eventually you find someone who will completely turn your world around. You will tell them things that you have never shared with another soul and they will absorb everything you say and actually want to hear more. You will share hopes for the future, dreams that will never come true, goals that will never be achieved and you will share many disappointments life throws at you while in the warmth of each others arms. When something wonderful happens, you can't wait to tell them about it, knowing they will share in your excitement. They are not embarrassed to cry with you when you are hurting or laugh with you when you make a fool of yourself. Never do they hurt your feelings or make you feel like you are not good enough, but rather they build you up and show you the things about yourself that make you special and beautiful. There is never any pressure, jealousy or competition but only a quiet calmness when they are around. You can be yourself and not worry about what they will think*

Lynton Viñas:
Shadow in the Darkness

of you because they love you for who you are. The things that seem insignificant to most people become invaluable treasures kept safe in your heart to cherish forever. Colours seem brighter and more brilliant. Laughter seems part of daily life where before it was infrequent or didn't exist at all. An e-mail or instant message or phone call helps to get you through a long day and always brings a smile to your face. In their presence, there is no need for continuous conversation, but you find you are content in just having them nearby. Things that never interested you before become fascinating because you know they are important to this person who is so special to you. You think of this person on every occasion and in everything you do. Simple things bring them to mind like a pale blue sky, gentle wind or even a storm cloud on the horizon. You open your heart knowing that there is a chance it may be broken one day and in opening your heart, you experience a love and joy that you never dreamed possible.

Lynton Viñas:
Shadow in the Darkness

You find that being vulnerable is the only way to allow your heart to feel true pleasure that is so real it scares you. You find strength in knowing you have a true friend and possibly a soul mate that will remain loyal to the end. Life seems completely different, exciting and worthwhile. Your only hope and security is in knowing that they are a part of your life. These words write here describe a life of contentment, and they are prophetic in what they can manifest for you, because you deserve love.

As Lynton slept, back at the Chavez mansion, Robert looked out over the sleeping town, seeing through whirls of greyness the vague outline of what he had made of the place that was now in the palm of his hand. His desires all came to pass. The littered papers, the dust that had gathered on the window sill, the tarnished brass on the lock were part of the ugliness that went with the territory of grand master of all he surveyed. However, he was

J. Wayne Frye

Lynton Viñas:
Shadow in the Darkness

a fearful man on this night. He had just received a call on his cell phone with bad news from someone who had failed at a task.

Deep in his heart, old bells of fear were ringing again after so many years. They were the slurred grumblings of grief and pain which he had put behind him long ago. Dull echoes of hideous times and poisonous interludes were cascading through his mind.

His hands were trembling, his short breaths were making his chest rise and fall precipitously. All was not well he thought? There had been murder in the town for years and nobody knew it. People just disappeared to never be seen again. The constabulary was incompetent and simply did not care as long as they drew a pay check. Who were all these who flew in the veins of the town, coiled and revolved and dreamed, vanishing without trace? They were just the poor, so who cared.

Lynton Viñas:
Shadow in the Darkness

Oh, what a night thought Robert. This was a night that spoke of death and destruction, but whose death, whose destruction? He turned from the window and there was Blackman.

Blackman moved toward him slowly, smiling. He was in front of him now, staring into his eyes. They embraced and kissed.

Lynton Viñas:
Shadow in the Darkness

CHAPTER 9

RAGING DEN OF DEVIL WORSHIPPERS

As evening falls,

And the yellow lights leap one by one

Along high and dark walls;

And along black streets that glisten with rain,

The muted city is in a restless sleep,

As lies that killed dreams are uncovered.

The shadow of death will not rest

As the dynamic dynamo goes into action.

J. Wayne Frye   153

Lynton Viñas:
Shadow in the Darkness

Where do dreams go to die? They are killed by complacency. For the poor, they simply have no dreams as their aspiration is to survive another day in a world where those at the top rule with impunity. A myriad of secretly gliding lights lie bare in the grand scheme of things never shining on the truth, because the world is not a vey nice place. It is a place where greed rules supreme and those who dare question the way of things generally wind up pilloried and destroyed physically, emotionally, psychologically and financially. There is no tolerance for boat-rockers. Accept your lot in life, get on board and let the captains of capitalism sail you on the ship of exploitation. Mess with convention and you will be tossed into a sea of sharks that will devour your mind, body and soul.

Yet, within this cruel system of exploitation, walks a woman who will not bend before the winds of adversity. Viva Lynton Viñas!

J. Wayne Frye

Lynton Viñas:
Shadow in the Darkness

She awakened early and called her friend at the *Manila Times*, Gordon Perez. She filled him in on all she had found out, and he promised to call the National Bureau of Investigation and have a man dispatched to the village as quickly as possible to assist her in the investigation. Telling Lynton to wait when injustice was rampant was like telling a typhoon to change course. It might happen, but was not likely. Years later, Wayne Frye would immortalize her stubbornness again and again in his books. This was a woman who would not be denied when she was on the trail of evil.

The lovers, Blackman and Robert arose, they leered at one another and Robert said, "Failure guarantees discovery. What happened last night cannot happen again."

With grim determination, Blackman said, "You want something done right, do it yourself. I am on the job now."

Lynton Viñas:
Shadow in the Darkness

Lynton strolled into the street, as the usual morning activities unfolded. People were preparing for their daily struggles to survive. Lynton looked at the huge Chavez mansion at the end of the street and knew that therein lay the problem – too much was in the hands of too few. She once liked Blackman and Robert, always had, but that did not mean she looked upon their affluence and privilege favourably.

She looked at all the tired, worn faces about her, most emotionless in their longing for some justice in a world where it was only reserved for the privileged. Those faces were ready to laugh, but most of all to shed tears of misery in a world that was always crushing them and their dreams.

Lynton had been an accomplished dancer for many years. Her muscular calves flexed with tightness as she was walking down the street, with

J. Wayne Frye

Lynton Viñas:
Shadow in the Darkness

an incredibly grim determination to assault evil.

She thought of her dancing days. In her youth, she would smooth her hair, lace golden slippers, run through the door to dance once more. Hearing swift music like an enchantment would rise in her head, she would perform before a thousand eyes. Ah, those were golden days when she did not realize there was so much injustice in the world. Now, she knew that darkness always falls. The walls of hope grow not luminous or warm. Rather, the walls tremble and shake with the lives within them moving in misery. Those within the misery of poverty and an uncaring society yearn for light, but are only greeted with darkness. A thousand winding stairs leads nowhere; and one by one in myriads the oppressed descend through half-lit halls which reach no end. The journey is long and tedious and there is no rest for the weary. Lynton walked to the jail, still gazing at the mansion on the hill, where the privileged danced in incredible

Lynton Viñas:
Shadow in the Darkness

display of opulent splendour.

She was walking alone into the lions' den, and she knew that she might be devoured. There was rain in her mind, the rain of lost hope for that poor boy and how many others? There was rain in the dreams of so many, rain forever, rain in the sky of the heart, rain in the willows that dampened all hope, but this was the dynamic dynamo and she had with her the mighty raincoat of righteousness that wrapped her in that special warmth and assurance that, no matter what, she would go down fighting.

She walked into the jail and leaning back in his chair was the jailer. He looked so peaceful, so calm and so dead! Blood oozed out of a small hole in the side of his head and a pistol was on the floor. A few fragments of brain matter lay on the desk. Lynton had seen death many times, so she was not shocked. She sighed and sat down.

J. Wayne Frye

Lynton Viñas:
Shadow in the Darkness

Lynton surveyed the scene - so young, so beautiful, so intelligent, so thoughtful and so angry. Indignation began to rise within and she wrinkled the skin between her eyebrows. The dark secret was becoming clear now, and she had put herself in the middle of a firestorm. Yet, there was a quiet grace about her as she observed the jailer, whom she surmised, based upon the coagulated blood, had probably been dead for several hours. This was no suicide either. Why had he been eliminated? Then it hit her!

She walked over to the desk and it was gone, snatched by the killer, no doubt. Were they really that stupid? Did they not know she had seen it? Ah, no difference, she thought as she said out loud to no one but herself, "I am the next to be eliminated. In fact, I was probably to have been last night's first victim, but the supposed executioner was foiled by my deadly heels and quick thinking."

J. Wayne Frye 159

Lynton Viñas:
Shadow in the Darkness

In the mansion at the end of the main street, Blackman and Robert greeted two confederates. The four men were frantic, because a well-kept secret was on the verge of being discovered.

Lynton saw no need to report the crime. It would be discovered soon enough. What counted now was exposing the murderers of the young boy, Mr. Benez and the jailer. She would need help, but while waiting the arrival of the NBI detective, she needed to find safety, and that was a tall order when you were not 100% sure of anybody in the village.

She slipped out the back door of the jail, walked down the dark alleyway and thought of all the times she had faced danger before, but this was a special kind of danger. She had walked into a raging den of devil worshippers.

Lynton Viñas:
Shadow in the Darkness

CHAPTER 10

SOMETHING EVEN MORE SINISTER

Satan, the great tempter,

Can take many forms.

Is he the fallen angel

Or is the conniving banker

Who takes a widow's home?

Is he the politician who lies

And feathers his own nest?

Is he the Christian hypocrite

Who says one thing and does another.

J. Wayne Frye

Lynton Viñas:
Shadow in the Darkness

Is he the friend who smiles

While stabbing you in the back?

Is the devil each man who seeks

Privilege, power and embraces greed?

Is the devil the man who preaches

Patriotism but never puts his life on the line?

The devil is among us, because he is us.

The absence of darkness in a person does not suggest an abundance of light, for to know the light you must have known the darkness, and Lynton had seen far too much darkness in her life. Yet, she embraced humanity for what it promised, not what it was. Still, she knew that there were those who preferred the darkness to the light. Her next move would have to be bold and straight forward, because she knew death was afoot in the village as she was on the list of those who needed to be eliminated before the nefarious dealings of the cult of evil there could be snatched from the darkness and put into the light.

J. Wayne Frye

Lynton Viñas:
Shadow in the Darkness

Meanwhile, the four in the Chavez mansion broke up with a commitment to do what must be done to eliminate the thorn in their side named Lynton. Blackman and Robert were determined that she must be dispatched quickly, and the one who had failed in the attempt the night before, innkeeper Richard Sanchez, still smarting from the mighty kick to the groin, assumed that he would again be singled out to complete the task alone. However, the decision was made to lure her to an isolated place, where all four would simply beat her to death and toss the body into the lake. However, one of the four left the meeting with the determination to not harm her, because he knew that she carried the mighty sword of righteousness by her side, and that there would be those who would not rest until her killer was exposed. So, as the others prepared for the evil deed, he went back to his place and began hurriedly packing his belongings and intended to be gone within a few hours, leaving murder to those with whom he had formed an evil affiliation.

The beautiful lady was not afraid, but she did tremble a bit while thinking how she could avoid detection awaiting the arrival of the NBI official. She decided that waiting in Nangalisan might be the best option, so she sat out on the well-worn path she had used to bring her to the trouble she now faced. Could it lead her from trouble as well?

Upon her soft lips that had sometimes been kissed by those lucky enough to embrace her charms rested the sweet taste of morning dew. She moved cautiously on the well-worn path, seeming to sense that there might be mischief about.

The thin bead of the sun peeped though clouds that waxed and waned, and left her partially in the dark most of the time. There was a slight gust of wind periodically that rustled the leaves on the trees. There was an intense quiet that was disconcerting to her, as it seemed unusually out of place in the forest.

Sometimes, we can feel a coming calamity. Is it a second sense when the hairs begin to rise on our necks and we feel chills run up and down our spines? Slightly crouching as she walked, Lynton's lithe body could sense the spirit of anticipation as a feeling of dread titillated her inner most thoughts. She looked to her right and standing near a big banana tree, with giant leaves flapping in the breeze, hidden under the branches, only partially visible was that damn shadow again. It was not moving, just standing there in the dark covering provided by the tree. The eyes were partially visible in the darkening area where it stood. They gleamed as if pleading.

Had she not done all in her power to expose his killers? Was she not risking her life to see he received justice? She looked behind her expecting to see the miscreants of mayhem. Nothing was there. She turned her head toward the tree again and the shadow was gone.

Her lips moved faintly, her eyes moistened, and the calm hands formed a fist in anticipation. Suddenly, with a sigh, the quiet lady began to once again move forward, but then she realized she had made a mistake walking toward Nangalisan. She should have stayed among the crowds. There was safety in numbers.

She realized the village behind her was nearer than the one before her. She pivoted, sighed and headed back toward from whence she had come. She was in the sunlight now, as the trees became sparser and the clouds dissipated. Yet, she still felt she was not alone, and it was not the shadow that was skilfully moving in the clump of vegetation to her left. It was something even more sinister.

Lynton Viñas:
Shadow in the Darkness

CHAPTER 11
KICK ASS

The page is turned, the dream forgotten;
The music changes tone, you wake and remember
Deep worlds you lived before,
Deep worlds hereafter
Of leaf on falling leaf, music on music,
Rain and sorrow and wind and dust and laughter.
All now fade into the disharmonious
Realization that you are being stalked.

J. Wayne Frye

Lynton Viñas:
Shadow in the Darkness

The boy had died in agony,
Sacrificed to the Prince of Darkness,
The schoolteacher's neck snapped,
The jailor despatched with bullet.

Hear the footsteps of death,
Play a buzzing melody.
Tomorrow may not come.
Yesterday may be all you have.
Through soundless labyrinths of a dream,
You pass many doors before the pit,
Where the evil one dances.
Can you hear the music of death?
See hope fall, fall into darkness.
You move forward.
Hark, do not look back.
Something may be gaining on you.

She always walked where her heart led, but was it her heart leading this time or were there malevolent, sinister forces at play in the fields of of discontent upon where the seeds of evil had been sown? She had come searching for adventure, and found it, but not the kind of adventure for which she was looking. She had descended into a cauldron of darkness where worshippers of the devil had now marked her for annihilation in order to avoid dedication. The terror had slowly crept upon her. Yet, the warning had been there in the form of a shadow that she had seen move past her that very first walk down the very path upon which she now trod. No matter where she went, that shadow had offered her a warning, but it had also beckoned, for whatever it was could not rest, would not rest until the perpetrators of evil who had snatched life from it were brought to justice.

This slowly gesturing thing menaced her mind with its pleading. Images flashed in her head as trepidation swept over her in waves like mortals encoding mortal time. They brushed her like

Lynton Viñas:
Shadow in the Darkness

cascading water in a shower. The water was not cleansing. It was hot with the breath of death.

Knowing, as she inched ever forward in hopes of mingling with crowds in the village to forestall evil that lurked after her, she began reflecting upon what she knew. She had no remorse for seeking justice. Dreams can be madness, smiles can be deadly, promises can be like glass smashed on a stone and illusions can portend reality.

Lynton was a woman who never backed down from a challenge. She was already an incredible young woman but had not gained the notoriety that would make her a household name throughout the world as her renown would grow into a legend. Still, this was not a time to tarry, as she knew that she was not going to make it back to the village. There were evil ones stalking her, and she had to face reality. She turned to look behind her and shouted, "Show yourselves."

Lynton Viñas:
Shadow in the Darkness

The taking of a human life, even if it was evil, preys upon a person's mind for the shedding of blood, even in self-defence is not to be taken lightly by those with a conscience and love for mankind. She waited, waited there coiled like a snake ready to strike, for the response from those she knew were stalking her.

As she waited, as memories of her life flashed before her and she began projecting on a future of which she had always dreamed. She thought of the man's love she had always desired but for which she was always on an eternal search, never finding the unconditional love for which she craved.

The chords and discords grew as she wanted to face those who had brought death and evil to this place. Now she was growing furious, because they were playing with her, toying with her, trying to instil fear in her for the perverted ends that stirred their passions.

J. Wayne Frye   171

Lynton Viñas:
Shadow in the Darkness

"Enough," she shouted as she stayed in her coiled position, ready to fend off who or what might come at her. She did not have on her notorious high heels from hell for which she would become renowned, but the determination to defend herself and fight for justice beat within her like a symphony of defiance. This girl would not go quietly, meekly into the night.

Growing weary of the cat and mouse games being played, she decided to openly confront those she assumed were lurking about. "I know Blackman Perez. I know Robert Chavez. I know Richard Sanchez of the deviltry that you embraced in at least three murders, probably many more. I stand here in defiance to the evil you love. I am woman. I am strong. I am invincible, and I am ready to kick ass!"

J. Wayne Frye

Lynton Viñas:
Shadow in the Darkness

CHAPTER 12
GLORIFICATION OF SATAN

They were the phrases of defiance,
As she stood head unbowed.
Evil ones lurked in the shadows.
And another greater shadow stood to her right.
It was the shadow that had haunted her,
But she saw it now for what it was.
This was the shadow sent to warn her.
Others had not seen it,

Lynton Viñas:
Shadow in the Darkness

Because it was there for her,
Pleading for her help,
But it was also there as an omen
Of the evil that sought her death.

Robert stepped out from behind a banana tree wearing an insidious smile. "You are not kicking anybody's ass little girl. You should be very afraid."

Then Blackman stepped out from the opposite side with Richard Sanchez. They stood defiantly on the pathway, staring at her in silence.

Lynton had danced to the music of discontent often in her life, for those who know poverty's pinch must fight to survive. She had really been on her own since the age of three, as she learned that sometimes the child must be the adult in a family. She was still coiled, waiting for the attack from two who had once professed love for her.

Lynton Viñas:
Shadow in the Darkness

The unplumbed light of determination was the seed planted in her long ago, and it had grown into a mighty tree with branches of steel. She was looking for words but they would not come.

Sometimes seeking justice is a lonely battle
Through running ghosts of shadow,—leaping at it,
Lying in wait for it to spring up,
Spreading faint snares for it of sense or sound:
Until, suddenly, as if in a phantom forest,
You hear it, see it flash among the branches,
And scarcely knowing how, suddenly have it.
You can finally grasp it in your heart.
Well, it was so as she was now facing death,
Glimpsing a face in darkness, hearing a cry,
Remembering days forgotten, moods exhausted,
Corners in sunlight, puddles reflecting stars;
Until, when least of all suspected,
The thing resolved itself with words of admission,
When Blackman let her feel his evil with words.
He was not the man she once knew.

J. Wayne Frye 175

Lynton Viñas:
Shadow in the Darkness

He had become something loathing and hideous.
How could she have ever been friends with him?
Oh, and Robert was even worse, for he had
Actually interested her at one time,
Before the sunlight of affection faded.

"You think you are so damn smart," offered Robert as he stood motionless, but you could see he was preparing to sprang upon her.

The pathos of the moment was not lost on Lynton as she looked behind Blackman and Richard at a dark shadow lurking maybe 25 feet down the pathway. Robert glanced that way, but obviously saw nothing.

Lynton had played many a tune on the guitar and sang with passion. She had a rhythmic tone to her voice that modulated with purpose. She called up that modulation and all that passion as she delivered an admonition on the evil of these three.

J. Wayne Frye

Lynton Viñas:
Shadow in the Darkness

"You Robert and Blackman once had a passion for life I admired, but I fear it was always a passion that hid your evil intentions. You struck a match that lit a fire of evil that you embraced, and you are about to get burned by little old me."

The tune she was about to play was a symphony of retribution for the evil these three had perpetrated. She was going to pour from her fountain of righteousness a torrent, a pounding wave, a Tsunami of indignation for a young boy who had to sacrifice his life for their repugnant villainy.

Thousands of dreams revolve and fall and flow, but these despicable men had taken a young boy's dreams and crushed them to satisfy their evil. They had marched down the marble stairs of Robert's ostentatious mansion to that place of heinous wickedness and called upon the power of Satan to serve their vile interests.

Lynton Viñas:
Shadow in the Darkness

Her eyes were riveted now on the three as she scanned them standing there, preparing for battle. All three had knives in their hands. Long blades of steel flashed in the semi-darkness, as they began slow movement in her direction.

Green leaves blew down and the place became dark as a cloud covered the sun. A quiet, soft rain began to gently fall. A breeze stirred in the almost deafening silence of the moment.

Lynton was surprised that she had no fear. Rather, blood was rapidly coursing through her veins and a rush of adrenalin made her visualize in her mind the secret way down the secret alley of determination to which she had always walked with pride and determination. These three represented the darkness, but she was the beacon that lit the way to justice. A slow, methodical, disarming smile crept across her lips as the three looked on with disbelief.

J. Wayne Frye

Lynton Viñas:
Shadow in the Darkness

No sounds emanated from anywhere in the forest. Silence abounded. The three had edged their way closer, but that is what she wanted. She was luring them into her web, tightening the noose around their evil, and she was about to strangle the life out of their calamitous depravity. She stood her ground but noticed that Robert was now moving behind her. Blackman and Richard were in front of her. Her avenue of escape was to her left or to her right.

Was she about to die? She was young and wanted to live, especially since she had read Wayne Frye's book about the power of love between two people. She had not known the kind of love she wanted yet. For some reason, as she stood there facing death, she dreamed of the man she had always wanted, a foreign guy who would lift her up and put her on a pedestal. She remembered some more words she had read in one of Wayne's books and they haunted her.

Lynton Viñas:
Shadow in the Darkness

Vulnerability is the essence of romance. It is the art of being uncalculated, the willingness to look foolish, the courage to say, "This is me, and I'm interested in you enough to show you my flaws with the hope that you may embrace me for all that I am but, more important, all that I am not." Love is accepting someone for whom they are, not whom you want them to be. Love is a quiet acknowledgement of the worth you place on someone. It is, in the cold night air, taking off your coat and wrapping it around her, so she can stay warm. It is reaching out to her when she cries, and soothing her with words of comfort. It is showing her off, letting everyone know you have the most valuable treasure imaginable. Love is telling someone, even when they are disarrayed that they are beautiful, because you see inside them, not just what is on the surface. Love is letting that person know it with words as well as deeds. Saying you love someone is easy; proving it with deeds is much more difficult. Love is never judging her for

J. Wayne Frye

Lynton Viñas:
Shadow in the Darkness

her past, but rather, planning for her future. Love is not expensive gifts, but the little things that say how much she means to you. Love can be glorified silence, when you look at her that certain way that says more than words could ever convey.

As she faced death, she wondered if she would live to find that love she had always desired. As a child - lonely, hungry and mired in the throes of want, she dreamed, not of riches, but of love from a man who would bring her the calmness, the kindness, the warmth that she so brazenly desired.

She looked into the forest on her right and it was there, beckoning, motioning for her to follow him. The others obviously did not see it. All three lunged toward her at the same time, and as she ran to her right into a thicket, the dark shadow led the way through it, seeming to float above the ground rather than walk. She heard the evil ones behind her, but did not look back.

Lynton Viñas:
Shadow in the Darkness

She recognized Robert's voice as he shouted, "You are dead. There is no escape for those who think they are righteous. Satan will destroy you!"

The words he muttered were walls that froze around her, but she still had the twilight of hope which beat a rhythm of defiance in her breast. She would still be guided by one dim light above her and hear far music, like a sea in caverns, murmur away at hollowed walls of stone where righteous indignation was her mighty shield. She bore within her heart the sorrow of those sacrificed to evil, and she was about to close the window of willowy wantonness that had been used to slay them.

She heard them behind her and before her the shadow danced through the thicket where branches and thorns were tearing at her flesh. How many times had she seen the shadow, thinking it a mechanism of evil? Yet, now she understood that

J. Wayne Frye

Lynton Viñas:
Shadow in the Darkness

it was only begging, pleading with her to exact justice for its tortured soul. It was not there to destroy her, but to warn her of the doom that waited.

Her shredded blouse was tinted with blood, but she knew those behind her were bleeding too. They were bleeding the slime of their malevolent evil that she was about to halt.

In the briars and spindly trees, she lost sight of the shadow that had apparently disappeared now that she had been led to where the final battle was about to take place. She was a red rose of beauty, but the stem of that rose had prickly branches that were as deadly as a striking snake.

She was a nimble nymph of never ending cunning and wile, as with torrid fastidious footsteps she was fleeing from their approach, while she led them through thickets that caused murmurs of pain. Had they brought guns she would already be dead, but these were devil worshippers with ceremonial knifes that they actually believed should be used to kill in ceremonial glorification of Satan.

Lynton Viñas:
Shadow in the Darkness

CHAPTER 13
A BLOW FOR RIGHTEOUSNESS

Evil works overtime in a world based on greed.
The good are chased like the dust
That spreads before the wind;
And like tumbleweed before the whirlwind!
For evil ones have fed the earth with wickedness.

Beliefs in fairy tales woven by manipulators of those ignorant enough to place their faith in the

Lynton Viñas:
Shadow in the Darkness

hands of the purveyors of superstitious clap-trap make many suffer at the trough of stupidity. Lynton depended on neither devil nor God, but on herself. She was alone in this battle against good and evil, and win or lose, she would go down fighting until her last breath, because she knew not how to give up.

Lynton, lovely in flight, was soft like a gentle breeze as her torn garments exposed her limbs, and the prickly briars seemed to fondle her delicate but taunt brown skin as her black, silky hair fluttered about her shoulders. Madness had taken hold of her three pursuers, as their only aim now was total annihilation of what they saw as a fly in their ointment of evil.

The desperation of the three increased their madness and their speed. As when the hound sees the frightened hare flit over the plain with eager nose outstretched, and impetuousness seizes

Lynton Viñas:
Shadow in the Darkness

him while rushing on his prey, the thrill of the hunt takes hold of the soul. The three were obsessed with murder again, and their evil hearts longed to wield their knives into her soft flesh.

As they were overwhelmed with hatred and madness for the kill, Lynton's wily aims were materializing. They pursued relentlessly until Blackman, in the lead and so close he could smell the softness of her flowing hair, lunged at her with his knife. She sensed the coming plunge and parried to her left. Blackman only lunged into the air and tumbled face-down forward into briars as Lynton now moved through the thicket on her left. Lifting him, Richard shouted obscenities in Lynton's direction as the three continued after her.

Lynton's own strength was becoming spent, as she grew pale and faint, but she knew she had more physical strength and will-power than her pursuers. A clearing was ahead, and a renewal

Lynton Viñas:
Shadow in the Darkness

seized her body as mighty determination closed around her gentle bosom, and her arms were like flailing wings flapping on a primeval bird of prey. Her churning feet were as swift as a gazelle sprinting across the plains of Africa. There was an aura that shone about her as this was the woman who transformed darkness into light. She was the beacon of hope in a world of hopelessness. She was the sword of vengeance for he who had been relegated to lurking about as a shadow hoping that someone might free him from his torment.

There are times when you know that the stars are perfectly aligning for you, and that everything is going to work to your advantage. Lynton's three determined pursuers assumed they had all the advantages. They had offered a human sacrifice to Beelzebub yearly ever since they were 16, and their last sacrifice was a 15 year old boy who had not rested quietly in the lake. These men had killed him, and then killed two others to cover up

J. Wayne Frye

Lynton Viñas:
Shadow in the Darkness

their crime. All that threatened their exposure now was if Lynton lived.

She had never embraced religion, because she saw it as an extension of corporate control of people's lives. To her, the church was just another corporation using people to increase its bottom line. It encouraged people to be fruitful and multiply, but after the babies were born made no effort to encourage the government to provide the children with shelter, food, health care and an education. Grand edifices were built to the glory of God, but the doors were locked except for Sunday services. While people went without shelter, ornate pews sat empty in cavernous churches. What would Jesus have done with those empty pews?

These men chasing her also had a religion, a religion that glorified the Prince of Darkness, and they saw humanity as a tool, just like the church did, to serve their ends. Worshipping God or the devil was not about the glorification of a good or evil deity. It was about what worship would bring you, whether it be eternal life in the hereafter in heaven where the streets were paved with gold or in the here and now where the rich and privileged enjoyed lives of splendorous excess.

Lynton had a purpose to leading the men ever further into the brush. It was not just the shadowy entity or the pursuers that had propelled her, because she knew from the beginning where she would lure these three so that she might have maximum advantage in the confrontation that was about to occur. She was a diminutive 5:2 and weighed only 50 kilos, but her heart was ten feet tall and weighed more than the Empire State Building.

Breathing hard and shallow, a sudden clearing appeared and she saw her goal. There, maybe no

Lynton Viñas:
Shadow in the Darkness

more than 25 feet away was the house of infamy where a young boy's life was sacrificed to the glory of Satan.

Inside, she would have the element of surprise. She heard the three shouting something incomprehensible at her, as she felt a rush of wind from a knife thrown at her back. It whizzed by her left ear, brushing her hair. She wanted to pick it up and use it in her defence, but she had no time to bend down, for they were hot on her trail, and halting would have given them the advantage.

She scurried into the house and up the stairs. They were in hot pursuit, but their carelessness was what she depended on to give her an advantage. Upon reaching the top of the stairs the three stood, glaring at the room where they had made a human sacrifice of a 15 year old boy. With hand gestures, Robert signalled for Richard and Blackman to enter.

Lynton Viñas:
Shadow in the Darkness

Stepping into the room while Robert moved to one side of the hallway and waited by the door, guarding it in case Lynton tried to escape, the two were greeted by emptiness. They surveyed the scene cautiously, but she was nowhere in sight. They stood in the middle of the room with looks of bewilderment on their faces. Meanwhile, Lynton was about to deliver a blow for righteousness.

CHAPTER 14
TO HIS DEATH

Lynton was a woman apart.
She had invisible wings
That let her move in slowly wreathing
Deliberate, intricate, silent patterns.
Plane upon plane, depth upon coiling depth,
Righteousness indignation boiling within,
Vaulted twists and curves and spirals
Were about to lay evil low.

J. Wayne Frye   193

Lynton Viñas:
Shadow in the Darkness

In a monstrous jungle of monstrous evil, Lynton was poised to rain a torrent of retribution upon the evildoers. They looked at the window and realized that they had not checked outside. They were not cautious enough in their pursuit.

They simply walked over, expecting to find nothing and they did, but when Richard leaned out the window, he did not bother to look up where Lynton had pulled herself onto the small upper ledge of the window that extended about 10 centimetres. With her small feet it was easy to turn to the side, put one foot in front of the other and stand on the upper sill of the window. When he leaned out, she leaped onto his neck, breaking it instantly. As he collapsed in death, she reached down and grabbed his knife before it dropped from his hand. Sitting on his neck, she wielded it viciously from left to right; right to left, as Blackman stumbled backward, falling to the floor. She leaped through the window, stepped on

J. Wayne Frye

Lynton Viñas:
Shadow in the Darkness

Blackman's hand that was still holding the knife, and you could hear the loud breaking of bones as he screamed in agony. As he tried to get up, he exposed his neck and she swiftly cut his throat.

Meanwhile, Robert stepped into the doorway, and Lynton gave a mighty toss of her knife in his direction. It buried itself deeply in his left shoulder and he screamed, turned and moved quickly out of the doorway, still carrying his knife by his side. She reached down, picked up Blackman's knife and moved cautiously toward the doorway. She stood by the door, fearful that he was waiting there near the top of the stair landing and would lunge at her when she stepped into the hallway.

Death waited, as Lynton dripped perspiration.
She was breathing heavily from exhaustion.
She sucked in as much air as possible,
Holding her breath to listen for Robert.
She heard him breathing heavily

J. Wayne Frye   195

Lynton Viñas:
Shadow in the Darkness

From fear and the physical pain.
She could wait him out maybe,
But she decided to make her move.

There are moments when you instantly know that you have made a mistake, and this was one of those moments for Lynton. She stepped into the hallway, facing the top of the landing, knife in her right hand held perpendicular to her shoulder.

Robert had stepped down on the first step, and she was too far away to wield a deathly blow. He lowered his head and with the knife still buried in his left shoulder, rammed into her hard, knocking her off balance. She dropped the knife and fell backwards onto the floor.

A sinister smile pursed across his lips as he stood over her, knife in his right hand. She was helpless there before him. He moved to his left, to make sure she could not kick him down the stairs.

J. Wayne Frye

Lynton Viñas:
Shadow in the Darkness

He was really enjoying this, watching her lie there completely helpless. He took a deep breath and said something incomprehensible.

Lynton, not one ever given to the use of profanity, said, "Kill me then you cretin asshole. Go ahead."

There is something in us all, be it force, or will, or passion, or determination, that makes us refuse to bow before fear. Lynton was waiting for death, and she was looking it in the eyes, unafraid.

"You should have never come here Lynton. Walking into the village that day was the biggest mistake of your life. You cannot defeat my master."

Wind blows. Rain falls. The clock moves ever forward and tolls the hour of our death. Lynton was hearing the toll of her demise, and then, just

Lynton Viñas:
Shadow in the Darkness

as she was about to close her eyes and accept her fate, Robert looked behind her and fear was stamped on his face. Lynton rolled her head to the right side and also looked behind. There it was – the shadow standing in the hallway, slowing moving forward toward Robert, and this time she knew. Yes, she knew that he saw it. He let out a deafening scream, stepped backwards and tumbled down the stairs to his death.

J. Wayne Frye

EPILOGUE
THE TORN PIECE

At the end of our exploring
we shall not cease from exploration,
and the end of all of our exploring
will be to arrive where we started
and know the place for the first time.
After the game is before the game.

"You are a helluva woman," said the inspector.

J. Wayne Frye   199

Lynton Viñas:
Shadow in the Darkness

Lynton grimaced as the paramedic tended to her wounds. She sighed and replied, "I actually lured them into a trap subconsciously perhaps, but still lured them. I thought two of them were even my friends."

They were in the jailer's office as they went over all that happened. The NBI Inspector was in obvious awe of this remarkable woman. "The world is rid of some of its evil today thanks to you. There will be an inquest of course, and no doubt a myriad of investigations, but be assured that you are never going to be charged with any crime. A few people are now coming forward with indications that they knew something was going on, but by virtue of Chavez's exalted station in life, they all feared what might ensue if they went to the authorities. That is, unfortunately, the way of the world in which we live. There are two sets of rules – lax rules for the haves and stringent rules for the have-nots."

J. Wayne Frye

Lynton Viñas:
Shadow in the Darkness

Lynton sighed again, as she said, "Truer words were never spoken, Inspector."

The whole village was abuzz with news of the horrible happenings at the old house off the pathway to Nangalisan, and a throng of people were standing outside the jail as Lynton walked out. They broke into spontaneous applause, and she humbly bowed her head. The inspector offered her a ride to Nangalisan, but to his surprise, she said, "I know you will think me crazy, but I think I'll walk through the forest to the main road and catch a Jeepney."

He smiled and said, "Stay out of trouble."

She had only walked a short distance when she came upon the church and noticed Father Mendez frantically packing his car. She walked over to him and said, "You leaving this parish for good father?"

Lynton Viñas:
Shadow in the Darkness

"I am, yes. My work here is done, and I think you for exposing the evil that had incubated and grown here. You have done a great service to the village. I am retiring, moving to Palawan."

"Evil will never be defeated father, because as long as men thirst after money, power, fame and glory, nothing will ever be able to corral the evil to which men are willing to go in order to obtain those things. Have a nice retirement father," she said as she started to slowly walk away. While she was doing so, she instinctively reached into her blouse pocket and fondled the little piece of black material she had found in the door jam of that evil house. Then she turned and looked back. Father Mendez waved goodbye to her, and she noticed that on the sleeve of the black cassock he was wearing there was a very small tear. She fondled the cloth in her pocket again and wondered, and wondered and wondered.

THE END OR IS IT?

J. Wayne Frye

Lynton Viñas:
Shadow in the Darkness

DON'T MISS THESE

EXCITING LYNTON ADVENUTRES

(Listed in Correct Sequence)

Lynton Curls Her Hair

Lynton Buys a Cell-Phone and Hears the Voice of Doom

Lynton Walks on Water

Lynton and the Vampire at Tagaytay Manor

Lynton and the Ghosts at the Mansion on Balete Drive

Lynton Viñas and Beowulf Perez: Demon Fighters

Chablis and Lynton in the Room of Doom
(For Adults)

Pursuit
(For Adults)

Lynton Viñas: Demon Fighter in Black and White
(For Adults)

FOR EXCITING SPORTS ADVENTURES TRY
THESE WAYNE FRYE BOOKS

How Hockey Saved a Jew From the Holocaust

Hockey Mania and the Mystery Of Nancy Running Elk

J. Wayne Frye   203

Lynton Viñas:
Shadow in the Darkness

VOCABULARY (Merriam-Webster Canadian)
(Definitions as they relate to usage in this book)

Prologue – 5

writhed - twisted
nonchalantly – in an unconcerned manner
crescendo – gradually increasing
trepidation – feeling of alarm
tranquility - peaceful

Chapter 1 - 11

promulgates – to proclaim
exalted – high regard
obscurity – not well known
trumped – topped or to be better than
trek – difficult trip
phenomena – remarkable development
denizens – person inhabiting a certain space
manifestations – an appearance
paranormal – outside normal sensory channels
scampering – rushing hastily
morphed – to change (often referring to shape)
postulated – to assert or propose
premonition – feeling something is going o happen
scurrying – hurrying about
uproariously – very funny
dynamo – person full of energy
respite - rest
paradoxical - contradictory
attributed – assigned to or resulting from
demonology – study of demons
abominable - awful
credence – confidently beleived
adjunct – something added to
enthralled - captivated
transfixed – concentrated in amazement
void - emptiness
silhouette – two dimensional representation of an object
benign - favourable
solace – comfort, relief

J. Wayne Frye

Lynton Viñas:
Shadow in the Darkness

Chapter 2 - 29

regale – to entertain with delight/capture attention
perpetually - continuous
contrive – to plot or plan with great thought
laborious – requiring much work
moniker – a nickname or alias
laissez-faire – free from interference, feeling of freedom
banter – exchange of light, playful talk
disconcerting – confusing or upsetting
trodden – past tense of tread/walked on a lot
obliterated – removed or destroyed
indistinguishable – unable to recognize
feverous – high intensity
tarry – not be in a hurry/hang around
stupefaction – overwhelming amazement
indignation – strong displeasure
cower – to crouch in fear or shame
hierarchy – ranking of one abobe another
abject – utterly hopeless
facetiously – not meant to be taken seriously
indolence – to avoid exertion
cadre – trained or qualified/a framework or outline
shenanigans – deceit, trickery, mischief, pranks
frivolous – not serious
mesa – steep walls with a flat surface on top
musing – contemplation/refelction
vainly – unsuccessful/without hope
hovels – dirty, substandard dwelling
periphery – on the outside of
respite – rest from
furtive – sly, shifty
embellishment – a fictitious addition to something
aggrandized – made great
bounty – generous gift or rward
studiously – carefully planned or maintained/hard study
deferential - respectful
abrasive – rude or inconsiderate

Chapter 3 - 57

Lynton Viñas:
Shadow in the Darkness

profusely – done freely or abundantly
quadrangle – with four angles or sides
mundane – common or ordinary
belabour – persistence in an argument
emphatically – forceful, insistent
discombobulated – confused or upset
overwrought – excessively excited
connivance – encouragement of conniving to do soemthing
impeccably – flawless, almost perfect in manner
cosmopolitan – belonging to the world rather than parochial
irreverently – not respecting
melancholia - sadness
permeate – to pass into or overwhelm
palatial - luxurious
ostentatious - luxurious
stalactites – deposits hanging from the roof of a cave
stalagmites – deposits reaching upward from cave floor
terracotta – clay-based earthenware
precipitous – very steep and usually treacherous
Chapter 4 – 77
inordinate – uncontrolled, disorderly. large number of
suffice – enough, adeqaute
unscrupulous – unrestrained, unprinciupled
countenance – facial expression, composure
Chapter 5 - 91
agnostic – existence of God unknown and questioned
astral – pertaining to the stars/on a higher plain
impudence – shameless, disrespectful
blasphemous – profane or irreverent
seditious – rebellious behaviour
acrimoniousness – bitter acting in speech or behaviour
amorous – showing or expressing love
apparitions – supernatural appearance of a person or thing
emanating – to emit, flow out
undulating – to move with a wave-like motion
myriad – a great number of
nymphs – beautiful or graceful young woman
abominable - awful

J. Wayne Frye

Lynton Viñas:
Shadow in the Darkness

insatiable – cannot satisfy
insidiousness – treacherous or decitful
perpetrated – to present or excute
malignancy – malignant behaviour or action/bad
excised – imposed or can be an elimination in some cases
pentagram – a five pointed star/can eb considered evil
luminous - bright
cascades – descending or falling over
defiled – to make foul or dirty
seethes – high agitation or excitement
shrilly – high pitched/intense/keen
Chapter 6 - 111
elfin – small, spritely, mischievous
tempests – stormy/very violent
infrastructure – framework or features of an organization
tumult – violent or noisy commotion
pallor – unusual paleness or fear of death
dissipated – broken up
sinuous – many curves, indirect, bending, lots of turns
dilates – spread out, expand
expendable – not worth keeping or maintaining
despondent – hopelessness, dejection
Chapter 7 - 131
sauntered – a leisurely walk or gait
fermented – agitate, create unrest
condescending – superior thinking and looking down
mundane – common or ordinary
sordid – dirty or filthy in manner
precipitously - very steep
forte – expert at
parried – to turn aside
excruciating – very painful to the extreme
coup-de-grace – finishing or decisive ending or action
Chapter 8 - 143
surly – rude, bad tempered, dark, gloomy
languor – lack of spirit, interest, vitality
pugilistic – person who fights with fists
weft – woven, generally in regards to fabric

Lynton Viñas:
Shadow in the Darkness

complacency – a quiet acceptance of things
malevolence – malice, hatred
constabulary - police
Chapter 9 – 153
aspiration – strong desire
impunity – exempt from punishment
pilloried – to expose to public ridicule or abuse
indignation – strong displeasure
surmised – to think or infer
coagulated – changed from liquid to a thickened mass
Chapter 10 – 161
waned – to decline in strength or intensity
nefarious – very wicked
lithe – limber, flexible
miscreants – vicious, depraved, villainous
mayhem – random or deliberate violence or disturbance
Chapter 11 – 167
disharmonious – not in harmony
cauldron – large kettle or boiler
annihilation – completely destroying or defeating
portend – to indicate, signify, an omen
Chapter 12 – 173
pathos – quality or power of a life experince
repugnant – offensive, distasteful
ostentatious – very showy in an attempt to impress
heinous - awful
vile – very bad or offensive
calamitous - disastrous
depravity – disgusting actions
disarrayed - disordered
throes – sharp attack or emotion
willowy – tall, slender, graceful
wantonness – deliberate without being provoked
cunning - shrewd
wile – trickery, artful
torrid - passionate
fastidious – excessively critical or particular
Chapter 13 – 185

J. Wayne Frye

Lynton Viñas:
Shadow in the Darkness

clap-trap – pretentious but insincere language/actions
trough – a long box-like receptacle for water or food
flit – move lightly or swiftly
impetuousness – sudden or rach action
primeval – relating the first age of the world
aura – distinctive quality or atmosphere
Beelzebub - Satan
edifices – a large size building
cavernous – deep set, large as a cave
infamy – extremely bad conduct
Chapter 14 - 193
torrent – rushing, violent inundation of anything
perpendicular – straight up or down
Epilogue - 199
inquest – legal inquiry
exalted – raised, elevated, lofty
stringent – convincing or forcible
abuzz – fully alive, full of activity
spontaneous – natural impulse
incubated – to hatch or develop